Double-Crossed in Gator Country

Double-Crossed in Gator Country

ERNEST HERNDON

ZondervanPublishingHouse
Grand Rapids, Michigan

A Division of HarperCollins*Publishers*

Double-Crossed in Gator Country
Copyright © 1994 by Ernest Herndon

Requests for information should be addressed to:
Zondervan Publishing House
Grand Rapids, Michigan 49530

Library of Congress Cataloging-in-Publication Data

Herndon, Ernest.
    Double-crossed in Gator Country / Ernest Herndon.
        p.   cm. (Eric Sterling, secret agent)
    Summary: Twelve-year-old Eric and his friends are sent by the CIA to
foil alligator poachers in the Everglades.
    ISBN 0-310-38261-0 (paper)
    [1. Adventures and adventurers—Fiction. 2. Alligators—Fiction. 3.
Poaching—Fiction. 4. Everglades (Fla.)—Fiction.]
I. Title. II. Series: Herndon, Ernest. Eric Sterling, secret agent.
PZ7.H43185Do   1994
Fic—dc20   93-44163
                                                                      CIP
                                                                       AC

Edited by Dave Lambert
Cover design by Jim Connelly
Cover illustration by Jim Connelly
Internal illustrations by Craig Wilson, The Comarck Group

Printed in the United States of America

94 95 96 97 98 99 00 01 02 /❖LP/ 10 9 8 7 6 5 4 3 2 1

For Lauren and Cole

1

"Remember!" Miss Spice called across the water. "If you get into fast water, trust your canoe!"

"What's she talking about?" I asked my buddy, Erik K., as the canoe the two of us were in glided down the stream.

He shrugged, grinned, and dipped his paddle into the clear water.

I looked back over my shoulder. Miss Spice's canoe cut through the water in a straight line. She sat in the rear, paddling expertly. Her thick orange-brown hair fell onto the shoulders of her crisp blue shirt. In front, Erik K.'s sister Sharon tried the new strokes Miss Spice had just taught us. With her paddle moving smoothly, and the sunlight in her golden hair, she looked eager and excited.

Erik K., who was thirteen, a year older than Sharon and me, was every bit as excited. Sitting in the back of our canoe, he was paddling hard and fast. Unfortunately he seemed to steer us at every fallen log in the river.

Bam!

"Not so fast, Erik!" I called back to him as I used my paddle to push away from a log. "We're leaving them behind."

"So? We already know how to canoe."

Well, we'd had one lesson. Earlier that morning Miss Spice had taken us out on a small lake and showed us how to put on a life vest, how to sit in a canoe, how to hold a paddle, and how to do the bow stroke, draw, and sweep. We'd practiced more than an hour. I guess that made us experts.

Now we were trying our new skills on this pretty, tree-lined creek.

"Watch out for that log!" I shouted.

BAM!

"Slow down, Erik!" I begged.

"Oh, calm down, Eric," he replied. "This is supposed to be fun."

Yeah, that's right—we're both named Eric. Only his ends with a K and mine with a C. That's why, when we're both around, people call us Erik K. and Eric C., so we'll know who they're talking to. To make matters worse, we have almost the same last name—I'm Eric Sterling and he's Erik Stirling.

"Hey—listen," I said. "Isn't that Miss Spice, yelling for us to slow down?"

"Nah, that's just the wind," he said, propelling us even faster.

By now Sharon and Miss Spice were nearly out of sight behind us, and they disappeared completely when we rounded a bend.

"Why is Miss Spice teaching us to canoe, anyway?" I asked.

"Who cares? It's fun, isn't it?"

"Yeah, but there's got to be a reason."

Erik K., Sharon, and I were agents for WSI—Wildlife Special Investigations, a branch of the CIA that sent us on secret missions to protect wild animals. In fact, it was the similarity of our names that tied us all in with WSI in the first place, through a crazy mix-up—but that's a long story. With school out for the summer, we knew that our boss, Miss Spice, would have some kind of assignment for us. But we didn't know what.

"Look out!" I shouted.

Bam! Bam!

We slammed into a logjam. This time it took both of us to push off.

"No problem," Erik said. "Man, this canoe is more stable than I thought! Wonder if I could stand up in it?"

"Don't try it!" I pleaded.

Ignoring me, he rose slowly to his feet. I grabbed the sides of the boat as it rocked from side to side.

"See?" he said. "Nothing to it."

Of course, having a black belt in karate, Erik K. had good balance. As for me, I had a hard enough time standing up on dry land without tripping over my own feet.

Just then the canoe slid over a hidden limb, tilting us toward one side. Erik threw his weight first to one side and then to the other, trying to keep his balance. One of his feet shot out to the side.

"Whooooaa!" I moaned, expecting to plunge into the river any second.

At last he dropped to his knees, just in time to keep us from flipping.

"Erik, cut it out!"

"Okay, okay," he grumbled. He slid back onto his seat and began paddling steadily, like Miss Spice had taught us.

"Let's slow down so they can catch up," I said.

The boat moved lazily in the quiet water, which reflected the blue summer sky and the green trees overhanging the banks.

"You know, you're right," I said. "Canoeing *is* fun."

"Easy, too," Erik said. "Kind of boring sometimes, though."

I smiled. Erik liked action and challenge. He'd gotten plenty of it on our first (and, so far, only) mission for WSI, on Lizard Island. Personally, I'd choose boring over dangerous any day.

Behind us, Sharon and Miss Spice came into sight. I waved, and they waved back.

I glanced at Erik K. A lock of brown hair fell across his tanned forehead. His muscles rippled under his T-shirt. "Do you like this as much as karate?" I asked him.

He laughed and shook his head. "No way. It's good for the arms, but—hey, up ahead! Rapids!"

I looked—white water rushing among logs and roots. I suddenly realized that I'd been hearing the noise getting louder for the past minute or so.

"Hold on tight, I'll steer us through!" Erik K. shouted. "You push us off if we start to run into anything!"

We passed through a narrow channel between two boulders, and immediately slipped into a long stretch of bumpy water where roots and rocks stuck up like teeth. My heart raced as the river picked up speed. Erik tried to guide us, shouting out something every now and then that I couldn't understand, but within a few seconds it was clear that we were totally out of control. As the stream curved, the current swept us toward the shore and under some overhanging limbs. Panicked, I grabbed a branch—and immediately understood that that was the wrong thing to do. Our canoe, pulled sideways, began to lean upstream, and water surged into the boat.

In an instant Erik K. and I were plunged into the ice-cold creek!

2

We came up spluttering and shaking water out of our hair and eyes. The current pushed us several yards downstream before we managed to find footing in the swift, waist-deep water; our canoe was hung up in a snag nearby.

Sharon laughed as their canoe approached. We glared back at her, not in a laughing mood.

"You boys pull your canoe to the bank and empty it," Miss Spice said calmly, trying not to laugh. "Then you may join us."

"You two look so funny!" Sharon said, pointing at us as her boat glided safely by.

Erik snarled at her. Then we found our paddles, dragged our canoe to shore, and emptied it.

"Man, that water's cold!" Erik said.

"You call that steering?" I said. "Why'd you let us run up under those branches?"

"If you hadn't grabbed 'em, we'd have been all right," he said. "You're the one who didn't trust the canoe."

"What was there to trust? We were totally out of control!"

"You boys quit arguing and come on if you don't want to be left behind," Miss Spice called.

We hopped back in, paddled out into the current, and hurried to catch up.

As we pulled alongside, Miss Spice said, "Maybe you should try practicing the things I've taught you."

"Like I'm doing," Sharon said with a grin. I made a face at her when Miss Spice wasn't looking.

A few minutes later we all reached the boat landing.

"All right," Miss Spice said, as we all pulled our canoes up. "You all did fine. Sharon, you need to pay more attention to your own paddling and less to the mistakes of others."

Erik gave Sharon a wise-guy look and snickered.

"Erik K., you have a strong stroke. You need to harness that power and think about where you want the boat to go—and to remember that canoeing, like karate, is a discipline with skills that need to be mastered."

"Yes, ma'am." Erik scowled, watching Sharon grin back at him, her nose in the air.

"Eric C., your paddling looked okay, but I'd like you to show a little more confidence—in your boat and in yourself. And both of you boys need to calm down and quit acting so rowdy." Miss Spice ruffled our hair. "Now come on. Let's get cleaned up."

That afternoon we went to WSI headquarters downtown. A secretary brought a tray of muffins, bananas, and milk into Miss Spice's large office.

"What? No doughnuts?" I said. My sweet tooth always appreciated the tray of goodies Miss Spice usually offered us.

She smiled. "I decided I should take better care of my young agents, so I'm serving you healthier food."

"Mokay by mumff!" Erik K. grunted, his mouth full of muffin.

"These are delicious, Miss Spice," Sharon said, with a disapproving glance at her brother.

"Canoeing does make you hungry, doesn't it?" our boss said.

"Why did we learn canoeing, anyway?" I asked, peeling a banana.

"As you've probably guessed, it's because of your next assignment." She stepped to the wall and pulled down a map of the United States. "Have any of you ever been to Florida?"

"We went to Disney World one time," Sharon said.

14

Miss Spice nodded. "If you'll look south of there, down near the very tip of Florida, you'll see a big swamp." She circled an area with her finger.

"The Everglades!" I said.

"Very good, Eric C. That's exactly where you'll be going."

"Whoa," I said. "Hold on. Aren't there alligators down there?"

"Yes, but you'll learn a little about alligators before you go."

"Oh boy!" Sharon said.

Sure, leave it to Sharon to be crazy enough to *want* to hang out around dangerous, man-eating alligators. She *loves* wild animals. Her father's a veterinarian at the zoo, and often brings home sick animals to stay at the clinic behind the house. Sharon's as comfortable with a lion as I am with a house cat.

The thought of a mission in the Everglades didn't make me nearly as happy as it did Sharon. I could see it already:

First we'd get lost, then a jillion mosquitoes would eat us alive, and then the alligators would eat whatever was left.

"Don't worry," Miss Spice said. "We'll have other agents in the area. Besides, I have complete confidence in all of you. Now," she tapped the map, "the Everglades may seem big and scary, but in fact the swamp is quite fragile. Take alligators, for instance. True, they're powerful, but they're an easy mark for poachers."

"Poachers!" Erik exclaimed.

She nodded grimly. "One outlaw gang in particular is well on the way to wiping out the gators in a large area of the swamp. They're hunting them for their skins, which can be used for shoes and purses."

"How do they hunt gators, Miss Spice?" Sharon asked.

"Very simple. They go out at night and shine bright lights across the water. The gators' eyes glow red in the light, and the poachers shoot them with .22 rifles."

"Why don't game wardens just arrest them?" I asked.

"They try. And the laws are strict. But the Everglades is a big place." She pointed to a green area covering the southern part of Florida. "By our best guess, the poachers will have their next shipment of hides ready in about a week. Most likely a yacht will come in from the Gulf of Mexico and pick them up at night."

"Why don't you arrest them then?" I asked.

"Because we don't know where they'll be, or exactly when the boat will arrive." She rolled up the map. "That's why I need you kids. You'll pose as Scouts, out to earn merit badges by canoeing and camping in the Everglades."

Camping? Wait a minute. Did she say *camping*?

Out in the open down there in the deadly swamps where if you don't catch malaria, the gators have you for breakfast? Just the three of us?

"Have I got this right?" I asked. "You want us to, like, camp out in the open down there? With dangerous poachers around, who are probably armed?"

"I'm glad you brought that up, Eric C.," she said. "You're right about the poachers—they're armed and dangerous. You aren't to contact them directly, for any reason. But the last thing they want is trouble, and they'll have no reason to bother Scouts. You'll have a radio, and if you see any suspicious activity you'll radio our agents in Everglades City. They'll take it from there. I'm planning to meet with your parents tonight to explain your assignment to them. Any other questions?"

"Only about a million. What happens if we're eaten by gators?" I said.

She smiled. "Glad you asked." Punching a button on her intercom, Miss Spice told her secretary to send in a Mr. Boudreaux. In a few moments the door opened and a small man with dark hair and dark eyes came in. He wore faded blue jeans, a khaki shirt, and dirty white rubber boots.

"Mr. Boudreaux, meet my young agents," Miss Spice said.

He smiled. "How ya'll are? I'm Willie Boudreaux. I'm from Cocodrie, Louisiana." He patted his white boots. "Ever hear of Cocodrie Reeboks? Dat's what we call dese boots back home, 'cause ever'body wears 'em."

"Are you a Cajun?" asked Erik.

Mr. Boudreaux grinned. "Certified and sanctified, raised in de swamp. Grew up huntin' gators and cotching muskrat. I've et ever'thing from rattlesnake to armadillo. Long as I got my hunting knife and my old pirogue I can stay down in de swamp near-about forever."

"What's a pirogue?" Sharon asked.

"Dat's sort of like a Cajun canoe, *cheri*. Now, as I was sayin', I grew up wit' de gators. I've hunted and trapped 'em ever' which way, legal or not. But I done quit dat stuff, and now I'm workin' for de college."

"Mr. Boudreaux oversees an alligator research project," Miss Spice told us.

Mr. Boudreaux clapped his hands together loudly. We jumped. "So! You kids ready?"

"Ready for what?" I asked.

"Go meet my gators, dat's what!"

3

Mr. Boudreaux led us down a path into a grove of trees behind the college. Chain-link fence bordered the walkway.

"Look!" Sharon pointed down a hill to a small stream. On the other side of it lay two gigantic alligators.

"Come on, ya'll," Mr. Boudreaux said. We followed him through a gate and down the hill to the creek. He crossed it on a footbridge, motioning for us to stay behind, on the opposite side of the creek from the gators. He didn't have to ask us twice. To my surprise, he walked right between the two gators and knelt there. Then he put a hand on one of the creatures' backs. It hissed and slashed its tail.

Even through Erik, Sharon, and I stood across the creek from it, we jumped.

"Easy, boy," Mr. Boudreaux said in a gentle voice. "Dis is a new one," he told us. "We got him a week ago, and he's wild as hot pepper." He patted the other gator. "Now dis dahlin's been wit' us for years. She's my sweetheart."

The wild one abruptly grunted and crawled toward the stream—straight toward us. I got ready to run. But the gator slid into the water, turned, and swam a short distance to a small pool, where it sank until only its eyes showed.

"I thought gators were dangerous," I said. "You don't act afraid at all."

Mr. Boudreaux stood up and chuckled. "Dey are dangerous, ooh la. Not all de time, not even most de time, but it only takes once. Now dis wild one, I been keeping my eye on him. If he act up I'm gone run as fast as my Cocodrie Reeboks'll carry me. But you know, in all my years of foolin' wit' gators, de only time one got after me was a mama when I got near her babies."

"What happened?" said Erik as Mr. Boudreaux crossed the creek.

"I was settin' a trotline and I didn't know dere was a gator nest on de bank right behind my bateau."

"What's a bateau?" Sharon asked as we followed Mr. Boudreaux back up the hill.

"Shhh!" her brother said. "I want to hear the story."

20

"A bateau's a flat-bottom boat, sugar. It's bigger dan a pirogue. Anyway, 'bout dot time I hear a roar and a hiss and I look around and here she come, musta been thirteen, fourteen feet long. Let me tell you, I dropped dat line and cranked dat motor faster'n anything I ever done, ooh la! She chased me 'bout a mile down de bayou 'fore she turned around and went back."

"Wow! What about your trotline?" Erik asked.

"I gave de babies time to grow some 'fore I went back. Now, let's go look at sompin' else, sompin' even wilder dan a gator."

"Wilder than a gator?" Erik whispered to me. "Like what?"

We went through the gate, careful to close it behind us, and followed the path. Behind their chain-link fence, gators of all sizes lay still as logs under the trees. The trail led around a corner to another gate.

"Dis time I want you kids to stay dere," Mr. Boudreaux said in a low voice.

Curious, I peered through the fence to see a dozen or more three-to-four-foot gators dozing around a muddy pool. Opening the gate, Mr. Boudreaux slipped in, shut it quietly behind him, and tiptoed toward the reptiles.

Suddenly one of them lifted its head, spotting him. Rising up on skinny legs, it raced quickly toward him.

To my surprise, Mr. Boudreaux turned and ran back toward us. "Look out! Here I come!" He opened the gate, dashed through and slammed it behind him just before the thing reached us. The creature opened its mouth, which was white inside, and hissed as if to say, "Just wait till next time."

"Wow!" Erik said. "What made that gator so mad?"

Mr. Boudreaux laughed. "Dose ain't gators, dahlin." He pointed to a small sign on the fence we had not noticed. "Dose are what dey call de American crocodile. Mean? Ooh la!"

"American crocodiles?" Sharon frowned. "I thought crocodiles lived in places like Africa and India."

"True, *cheri*. But dey's one kind found in de United States. Dey not many left, and dey only in one place."

"The Everglades," I guessed.

Nodding, he motioned us back up the trail. As we walked, he explained that American crocodiles also live in Central America, can grow up to twenty feet long, and have been known to attack humans. The American alligator, on the other hand, lives only in the United States and is considered less dangerous.

"But how do you tell them apart?" I asked.

"Easy," Mr. Boudreaux said with a twinkle in his eye. "Just look at de teeth. When dere mouths are closed, you see a crocodile's bottom teeth sticking up, and you see a gator's top teeth sticking down."

"Who's going to hang around long enough to see his teeth?" I said, and Mr. Boudreaux grinned.

"What do we do if we run into a crocodile in the Everglades, Mr. Boudreaux?" Sharon asked.

"Oh, dere ain't much chance of that, child, seein' as how dey're so rare. But you might see some gators." Then he frowned. "Dat is, if de poachers haven't killed 'em all."

4

A couple of days later, we sat crammed together in the cab of a pickup truck in Florida with Mr. Rogers, a WSI agent posing as our Scoutmaster. He had just picked us up at the Miami airport. All of us wore Scouting uniforms, but as odd as I felt in mine, Mr. Rogers for sure looked the strangest—with his big gut and handlebar mustache, he looked like a reformed pirate.

We left the big city and entered a hot, flat land where high grass grew on either side of the road.

"The Everglades used to cover all this country," Mr. Rogers said, sweeping out a hairy arm. "Now it's disappearing. Farms and houses everywhere. Just look." He pointed to a humongous shopping center and subdivision still under construction; they seemed to stretch on forever. "Some people think the 'Glades may be gone in a few years."

"Why is that so bad?" I asked. "I mean, it's only swamp."

Sharon elbowed me. "Don't be dumb, Eric C. Animals live in the swamp."

Mr. Rogers nodded and sighed. "The less swamp, the fewer animals."

We entered grass country again. Erik pointed to a sign by the road. "What does 'panther crossing' mean? Is that a joke or something?"

"No joke, Erik K.," replied Mr. Rogers. "Ever heard of the Florida panther? There aren't many left in the wild, but there's still a few hiding out in the Everglades."

"But why a sign?" Erik persisted.

"One of the biggest killers of Florida panthers is cars. The cats roam a big area, and when they cross a highway like this, they can get hit."

"Gators, crocodiles, panthers," I mumbled, listing all the things that might get me.

"Don't forget sharks," Mr. Rogers said.

"Sharks!"

He chuckled. "The Everglades is bordered by the Gulf of Mexico, you know. Sometimes sharks swim into the rivers and bays." Then he patted my knee. "Don't worry, you kids will be fine. The sad fact is, the animals are in a lot more danger from people than the other way around."

We pulled into Everglades City, a small, sleepy town. Nearby, at the edge of a large bay, was the National Park office. Mr. Rogers stopped in the parking lot.

"This is where you'll start," he said. "They call this Chokoloskee Bay, and that island over there is Chokoloskee Island. Come on, let's see about renting a canoe."

A woman ranger led us to a fenced area where metal canoes were stacked. She picked out a long one for us, and gave us paddles and life vests from a storage shed.

"You kids are in for a hot trip," she said as we carried the boat to a small landing. "Not many people canoe this time of year. Too many mosquitoes."

"Great," I muttered.

"Also, watch out for thunderstorms," she said. "Lightning is a killer out here."

"Terrific."

We filled our water jugs at a faucet. Then we took bags of camping gear from the truck and tied them into the canoe. Finally Mr. Rogers unrolled a map on the hood of his truck.

"You'll want to follow the Wilderness Waterway," he said, tracing a line with his finger. "It's supposed to be marked. You'll go along this bay, around Chokoloskee Island and up Lopez River."

"Where do we camp?" Erik asked.

"Depends on what kind of time you make. The first night you might want to stay at Lopez River campsite. The next night you could camp on a chic-kee at Sweetwater Bay."

"Chickee?" Sharon giggled. "What's that?"

"A wooden platform for camping. The Park Service builds them where there's no high ground."

"How will we find the poachers?" Erik asked.

Mr. Rogers shrugged. "That's something no one can tell you. Just keep your eyes and ears open, and radio us if you see anything unusual. We'll have agents standing by."

As Mr. Rogers folded the map, Sharon climbed into the front of the canoe. I stepped carefully into the middle and stowed the map in a pocket of my pack. As Erik settled himself in back, I glanced over my shoulder; he was twitchy and grinning with excitement. But it wasn't excitement that kept my stomach churning—more like fear. How many dangers *were* there in this strange, wild place? Gators, sharks, lightning, armed criminals . . .

"Goodbye, kids. Good luck!" Mr. Rogers called, pushing us off.

We paddled onto the bay, where small waves bounced us up and down. Though the air was hot, the breeze felt cool. The three of us stroked in rhythm, but progress was slow against the wind with the heavily loaded boat.

"See, Eric?" Erik K. said. "This isn't so bad."

"As long as we don't turn over," I replied.

"Even if we do, the water's not more than three or four feet deep."

I stared down at the clear water. At that instant the bottom exploded in a cloud of sand. I felt something big scrape the underside of our canoe as a huge, dark shape swam away at lightning speed.

"What was that?" Erik K. said.

"I don't know," I said, "but it was as big as our boat!"

5

"Might have been a manta ray," said Sharon, frowning at the two rows of waves left by the fleeing creature.

"What's that? Like a sting ray?" I asked.

She nodded. "In the same family. The manta ray is one of the biggest fish in the world. When it lies flat on the bottom it's nearly invisible."

"Bet our canoe spooked it when it went over," Erik K. said. "We're lucky it didn't flip us."

I nodded. "That's another thing I can add to my list."

"What list?" Sharon asked.

"My list of things that might eat us."

"Oh, Eric C., manta rays don't eat people."

"Well, it looked big enough to."

"Really," Erik agreed.

We rounded Chokoloskee Island, where houses stood among low palm trees and boats were tied to docks. Then we headed toward an opening in the wall of low, dark trees.

"That must be Lopez River," Sharon said, studying the map I had handed her.

"Is it far to the campsite?" Erik asked. "I'm getting hungry."

"Yeah, and it's getting late," I added. "We need to camp soon."

"It shouldn't be far," Sharon said, folding the map.

At last we left the open water behind and paddled into the mouth of the river. Here, the water was muddy and still. The forest on either side of us looked unbelievably dense, with thousands of high, tangled roots that covered the mud. It would be impossible to walk through there.

"At least there aren't any mosquitoes," I said, my voice echoing in the eerie silence.

"Well, we have bug spray in case there are," Sharon said. Then she pointed. "That looks like the campsite."

A tiny white beach stuck out into the river up ahead, the only piece of dry ground in sight.

"That looks nice," I said. "Hey, there's even a picnic table, over there under the trees."

"All right!" Erik said. "Let's get supper cooking."

We landed on the beach, and Sharon jumped out. "Here's a flat place to pitch the tents," she said, walking into the woods.

Suddenly she turned and ran toward the boat, slapping at herself wildly. Mosquitoes covered her like gray gauze. But when she stepped into the sunshine on the beach they seemed to lose interest and float away.

"There's a million mosquitoes in there!" Sharon cried, rubbing her face, neck, arms, and hands.

"Here, let's put on our jackets and caps and use this spray," I said.

We put on the extra clothes, then sprayed each other with repellent.

"Ready?" Erik said.

We carried our packs into the grove. It was like walking into a storm, only this storm buzzed and swarmed.

"You weren't kidding!" Erik said, swatting wildly.

"Let's get the tents up!" I said.

Working together, we pitched the two shelters and threw our sleeping bags inside.

"Maybe we should skip supper and get inside," Sharon said.

"Are you crazy?" Erik said. "I'm starving!"

"Look," I said. "Most of the bugs are staying off because of the repellent." I held up my hand to demonstrate. The mosquitoes hovered right over my skin but didn't land.

Sharon waved her hands beside her head. "I still don't like the sound of all that buzzing. It's scary."

I quickly fired up the stove and we heated two big cans of stew. As it cooked, dozens of mosquitoes got into the pot and drowned.

"Mosquito stew. Mmmm," I said, spooning it out into bowls and passing them around.

"Hey—what's that?" Erik said, pointing toward the ground several yards away.

"Snake!" I said, jumping up.

A long, black speckled snake crawled across the ground among the trees, totally unafraid of us.

"Hey, there's another one," Erik said.

"Are they poisonous, like water moccasins or something?" I asked Sharon.

"I don't think so. They look like speckled king snakes." But instead of jumping up to check them out, as she normally would have, she shook her head wildly and swatted at the clouds of mosquitoes. "Guys, I've had it with these mosquitoes!"

"I know what you mean," said her brother, picking bugs out of his stew.

"It's those snakes that have me worried," I said, keeping an eye on them. "Let's go out to the water."

I didn't need to say it twice. We all jumped up and hurried out of the woods into the sunlight. Sharon clawed at red welts on her neck.

"Somehow they've been biting me in spite of everything," she wailed. "And this jacket is so hot!"

Erik stared at the water longingly. "I say we jump in and cool off."

"Let's," Sharon agreed desperately.

But as they started pulling off their shoes and jackets, a large dorsal fin broke the surface just a few feet away.

"Wait!" I shouted. "Shark!"

Sharon took one look at the dorsal fin slicing through the water and burst into tears. "I hate this place!"

6

The fin went under, then came up again, and the creature blew water from a hole in its back.

"Hey," Erik K. said. "That's not a shark."

It raised its eyes out of the water then, and just the tip of its snout. Definitely not sharklike. "I think it's a dolphin," I said.

Sharon wiped her eyes and stared. "It is. It *is* a dolphin," she said excitedly, changing moods just like that. She squatted and held out a hand. "Hey, dolphin."

The creature raised its head, peering at us with curious eyes. Then it went under and disappeared.

"Maybe not everything's out to get us, after all," Erik said.

Sharon stood up. "I love dolphins." She laughed and wiped the tears from her still-wet cheeks.

Erik put his arm around her shoulders. "Come on, let's finish eating before the stew cools off. Then we'll get in the tents where the mosquitoes can't get us."

We stood by the water to finish eating, then quickly washed the dishes. As soon as the last dish was stowed, Sharon unzipped the mesh door of her tent, dove in, closed it swiftly—and immediately called out in frustration, "Oh, man! Look at all the mosquitoes that came in with me!"

"Use this," Erik said, offering her the bug spray, which she snatched quickly. Sharon sprayed a cloud of the stuff in her tent and handed the can back out to us.

"Our turn," Erik said, making a wry face. We plunged in, zipped up, sprayed the smelly stuff, and covered our faces till it settled. Finally we stretched out on our sleeping bags.

"Man, it's hot," Erik said after a minute or two.

"But we can't go outside," I complained. "Too many mosquitoes."

"Wish we could swim."

"With the snakes and the gators?"

He sighed. "Yeah, I know."

"Hey, I've got an idea," Sharon said from her tent next to ours. "I'll read out loud from this guidebook I bought back at the ranger station."

36

"Okay," said her brother unenthusiastically.

"Maybe it'll get our minds off our problems," I said.

"It's called *Everglades: Fact and Fiction*," Sharon said. "Here, listen to this. 'In addition to the many species of fish native to the park, biologists have found piranhas, the famous flesh-eating fish of South America.'"

"Piranhas!" Erik said.

"'Apparently, people bought the fish to keep in their aquariums, but when they got too big to keep, they released them into the swamp,'" Sharon read.

"I know we can't swim now," I said.

"Yeah, read us something more cheerful, sis."

"All right, I'm sorry," Sharon said, flipping the pages. "Here, this looks interesting. 'The Legend of Mr. Watson.'"

"Yeah, that sounds good." Erik said.

"'Many years ago, a mysterious man named Mr. Watson grew sugarcane deep in the Everglades,'" Sharon read. "'He hired drifters and hoboes to work his crop for him. Often these people never returned, and their bodies sometimes washed ashore at Chokoloskee Island.'"

"Great, we got dead bodies now," I grumbled.

"'Finally, the angry townspeople caught Mr. Watson and killed him, putting an end to the string of murders. But legend has it that the ghost of Mr. Watson still roams parts of the Everglades, looking for new victims.'" Sharon giggled. "Oops, sorry, guys. I didn't know it was going to be a horror story."

"This is a real fun place," I said. "We ought to charge admission. A hundred kinds of wild animals waiting to eat you up, and no extra charge for the ghosts!"

"Ghosts," Erik scoffed. "No such thing, buddy."

"Maybe, but there *are* poachers, and they have real guns!"

"Hey, this sounds neat," Sharon said. "Have you guys ever heard of the manatee?"

"What is it, some kind of evil Indian spirit?" I said.

"No, listen. 'The manatee, also known as sea cow, is one of nature's gentlest creatures. Although it may weigh more than a thousand pounds, the manatee feeds only on plants. It is possible that early reports of mermaids were in fact manatees. Though sea cows are anything but pretty, sailors may have thought these large creatures were mermaids. . . .'"

I closed my eyes listening to Sharon's voice. Just outside the tent, billions of mosquitoes sang hungrily. I imagined they were mermaids, singing sweetly to each other, and pretty soon I was fading, fading. . . .

* * *

When I woke, it was dawn, and much, much cooler. I noticed something right away. "No mosquitoes!" I said, peering out through the mosquito netting.

"What?" Erik mumbled sleepily, his voice muffled by his sleeping bag.

"The mosquitoes are gone!" I unzipped the door, went out, and stood there for a moment. Nope. Not one mosquito.

Suddenly something bit my neck. "Ouch!" I swatted, then scratched. There was a sharp bite on my hand next, and then my cheek. "What's doing this?" I grumbled. "I don't *see* anything."

"What are you griping about?" Erik asked, crawling out. Then he slapped his cheek. "Hey! What's biting?"

"I don't know." I grabbed the bug spray.

"Sand flies," Sharon said, slapping at her neck and face as she came out of her tent. "They're called no-see-ums because they're almost too tiny to see. I read about them in the guidebook."

The repellent didn't do much good against these pests. After a quick breakfast, we packed the canoe and paddled back onto Lopez River in the cool early morning.

"Boy, this is neat," Erik said in a hushed voice as we moved quietly up the tree-lined river.

"Look," I whispered. A pair of raccoons played among the tangled roots. They seemed to be having fun, wrestling and frolicking. Sharon giggled.

"Let's see how close we can get," Erik said quietly, steering the canoe toward them.

The coons didn't seem to notice us, even when we were only a few feet away. They tussled among the roots like kids at recess, then finally rambled away.

"I've never been that close to a wild raccoon," Erik said.

We followed the creek until it opened out into a huge lake. Holding our paddles out of the water, we drifted out into it.

"According to the map, we should see another marker for the Wilderness Waterway," Sharon said.

"I don't see one," I said.

Erik rose unsteadily to his feet in the canoe and scanned the distant shoreline, hand above his eyes. *He never learns*, I thought, remembering our experience in the river as Miss Spice was teaching us to canoe. *Hope he doesn't dump us all in, packs and all.*

Finally he sat back down. "I don't see one either. Which way should we go?"

7

"Wait a minute," I said, pulling my compass out of my pocket. "Which way is the marker supposed to be?"

Sharon checked the map. "Southeast."

Studying my compass, I pointed. "That way."

We paddled in that general direction. Before long, we spotted the tall white post marking the Wilderness Waterway.

"Good thinking, Eric C.," Sharon said.

"Yeah, that's using your head, buddy," Erik added.

Miss Spice had shown each of us how to use a compass. I didn't catch on very quickly to most of the things she had taught us, but for some reason, I understood compasses and direction. I seemed to have a knack for it.

As the sun grew hotter, we stopped to apply sunscreen. At noon, we tied up to some trees and ate lunch in the canoe.

"Boy, it's hot!" Erik said, munching a granola bar.

"At least there aren't any mosquitoes out here on the lake," Sharon said.

I swatted my arm. "Just these horseflies. Seems like there's some sort of bug for every hour of the day or night."

"And the spray doesn't work on these flies," Erik added. "You just have to whack 'em." Studying one that landed on his arm, he struck suddenly with the flat of his hand. "Got him! That makes thirty-two."

After lunch, we nestled against our packs and fell asleep in the shade. I woke to a rumbling sound —thunder! Black clouds billowed over the lake. Lightning flickered in the distance. A cool wind gusted across the water.

"Come on, gang!" I said. "Better get moving."

Sharon frowned. "Should we try to cross this lake with a storm coming up?"

"If we wait here, we might not make it to Sweetwater by dark," I said.

"I say we go for it!" said Erik, always ready for action.

"All right," Sharon said uneasily, "but let's paddle fast and get into the shelter of those trees on the far side."

We stroked quickly away from the patch of trees and onto the open lake. The wind slowed our progress, but after the morning's harsh sun it felt good. To our right, beyond the low line of trees, lightning crackled and thunder boomed.

"Faster!" Erik urged, obviously enjoying himself.

We dipped our paddles as swiftly as we could. Out here in the open, the wind had whipped the water into waves that rocked the canoe from side to side.

"Don't let the boat turn sideways into the waves," I said.

A long vein of lightning streaked the sky and thunder exploded overhead. A hard gust of wind blew our hair back, then the air became still as rain began to pepper the water in big shiny drops. I sniffed the sweet moist smell.

"I'll get our ponchos out," I volunteered.

"Wait," Erik said. "Let's get off the lake first, under those trees."

The rain fell harder, soaking my shirt. But it felt good, almost like jumping into a swimming pool on a hot day. Thunder roared again, and a last burst of speed took us to the end of the lake. We pulled up in a narrow channel under some overhanging branches.

We turned the canoe so that we could look back out over the lake and then just sat, breathing heavily. I rubbed my sore hands together. Now that we weren't working so hard, the rain dripping down through the branches felt cold.

"I'll take my poncho now." Sharon shivered.

I found them in our packs and we quickly bundled up, pulling our hoods up against the icy rain. The world had turned gray and wet. Thunder crashed on the lake behind us.

Slowly, the storm began to lessen. Instead of a sheet, I could see individual drops again. Finally it slowed to a *plop-plop-plop*, and I threw my hood back. A mosquito promptly buzzed at my ear.

"Boy, that was some downpour," Erik said.

"Thank goodness we didn't get fried by lightning," Sharon said. "It's scary being out in the open like that."

"How far to Sweetwater, Sharon?" I asked.

She looked at the map and sighed. "A long way. We'd better start paddling."

Many hours and many lakes and streams later, we turned up a wide creek.

"It's not far now," Sharon said. "We'll have plenty of time to make camp."

"Yeah, if we still have the strength," I panted.

Just then we heard a motorboat coming our way.

"Careful—could be poachers," I warned.

"Maybe it's just fishermen," Sharon said.

A small boat with two men came into view from behind some trees. They slowed as they neared us, and I relaxed when I saw rods and reels.

"Hey, kids," said the guy in front wearing a long-billed cap. "How's the fishing?"

"We're not fishing," I said.

"Not fishing? Why would anybody come to the Everglades and not fish?"

"We're Scouts," Sharon piped up, pointing to our uniforms.

The man nodded. "Camping out, huh? Where'd you stay last night?"

"Lopez River," Erik replied.

"Mosquitoes bad?"

"Were they ever!" I exclaimed.

The two men laughed and shook their heads. "Lopez River's the worst campsite in the 'Glades for mosquitoes," said the man in back, who wore sunglasses.

"We're going to Sweetwater tonight," I volunteered, then wondered if I should have told them.

The men nodded. "Camped there last night," said the guy in front. "Be careful. There's gators around that chickee."

"Gators?" I said. We hadn't seen any so far.

He nodded. "People clean their fish there sometimes. Gators hang out waiting for scraps."

"Is there anywhere else to camp around here?" I asked, suddenly reluctant to visit Sweetwater.

"Sure," the one in back said. "The Watson Place, a few miles west of here."

"Watson?" Erik asked. "As in 'Mr. Watson'?"

46

"Yeah. Heard of him? They say his ghost still lives here. Last few months, some people have heard shots at night and seen lights, and they swear it's the ghost of the old killer." He chuckled. "Just a tall tale. Well, you kids be careful." The men motored away.

The three of us sat in silence. Finally I said, "Well, which is it? Gators or ghosts?"

8

"I say we camp at Sweetwater," Sharon said. "That was our plan. Why change it now?"

"But the gators," I protested.

"That's why Mr. Boudreaux took us to the college, so we wouldn't be afraid of them," she argued.

Erik began to paddle, and Sharon and I joined in, heading up the creek, which was bordered by scrubby trees and bushes. Soon the creek widened and we saw a pair of wooden platforms standing several feet above the water. A roof covered each platform, and a walkway joined them.

"Hey, that looks neat!" Erik said. "No gator could climb up there."

"Wait," I said. "Look close to see if there's any around. They might get us while we're climbing out of the boat."

"Oh, Eric C.!" Sharon said, exasperated. "Even if there are, they won't hurt us!"

"Oh, yeah? Well, what about crocodiles?" I said, picturing a twenty-foot man-eating monster.

She didn't answer, probably remembering the hungry crocs at the college, and we approached the chickee slowly. But we didn't see a single gator or crocodile. At the chickee we tied the canoe and began unloading our camping gear. Soon we had our tents pitched side by side and beanie-weenies simmering on the campstove. In the west, the sun was sinking into the trees. The nearby forest hummed with insect noises.

"Boy, this is a lonely place," I said.

My friends nodded. They too were staring at the red sunset and the seemingly endless woods and water.

"And so big," Sharon said. "According to our map, we're just barely into the Everglades."

"And we've paddled two days!" Erik said.

"Beanie-weenies are ready," I announced.

As we ate, the sunset faded, and swarms of hungry mosquitoes joined us for supper.

"Uh-oh. They're here," Sharon said, quickly finishing her meal.

"Let's get in the tents," I said. "I'll wash these dishes."

I climbed down into the canoe, planning to wash dishes over the side. I was dipping a plate in the water when Erik said quietly, with excitement in his voice, "There's one. To your left, Eric."

Just a few feet away a small gator had surfaced, studying me with cold yellow eyes.

"It's just a baby," Sharon said. "See? It's only a couple feet long."

"Yeah, but what about his mama?" I said, quickly finishing the dishes and scampering back to the safety of the chickee.

Soon there were three little gators floating near the canoe, obviously looking for something to eat. Then they sank, vanishing without a ripple.

"Ugh. They give me the creeps," I said.

"I think they're cute," Sharon said. "It's the mosquitoes that drive me crazy."

"You don't think the gators can climb up here, do you?" I asked.

"Of course not." She slapped her neck.

"Let's get inside," Erik said.

Sharon scooted into her tent and Erik and I into ours, zipping the mesh doors shut behind us. It was too dark for Sharon to read to us, so we sat cross-legged on our sleeping bags, staring out at the darkening sky. Mosquitoes bumped against the tent's netting, trying to get in.

"I don't know about you guys, but I'm not sleepy," Erik said after a while.

"Me either," Sharon said from her tent.

"What else is there to do?" I said.

"Why not go out for a little float?" Erik asked.

"In the dark?"

"Sure. There's a moon out." He pointed to the nearly full disk of silver rising over the trees. "Should be bright enough to see. We wouldn't go far."

"Go ahead, then. But I think you're crazy."

"I'll go," Sharon volunteered.

"Great!" Erik said, slapping my arm. "Hold down the fort, big guy."

"Are you guys out of your minds?" I scolded as they hurried outside, spraying themselves with repellent and zipping up their jackets. "What about gators and mosquitoes?"

"The mosquitoes shouldn't be so bad out on the water, away from the trees," Sharon said. They settled into the canoe and pushed away from the chickee. "Don't worry, we'll be back soon."

Through the mosquito netting, I watched the canoe float gently away into the moonlight. The water glowed silver. Soon they rounded a bend and disappeared.

Lying back on my sleeping bag, I shut my eyes and tried to block out my fears. Mosquitoes bumped their noses against the mesh, wanting my blood. Now and then I heard little splashes—huge granddaddy gators trying to climb up and eat me alive, no doubt.

A twig snapped nearby, and I sat up. What was it? A panther, starved for fresh meat? Or the ghost of Mr. Watson, seeking a new victim?

Just calm down, I told myself, lying back. *Maybe the twig snapping came from some friendly raccoons, playing in the darkness. Maybe the splashes were dolphins. . . .*

I dreamed I was marooned on an island in the ocean. As I stared out to sea, a mermaid rose out of the water and began to dance. But she sure didn't look like I would have expected a mermaid to look. Her lower half was a dolphin, her upper half looked more like a cow, but with hands. She wore a long blond wig and had a raccoon mask across her eyes. She sang with a humming noise.

"Eric C.! Hey, Eric! Wake up!" It was Erik K.'s voice.

I opened my eyes and sat up. Erik and Sharon were in their canoe beside the chickee.

"Come see what we've found!"

9

Reluctantly, I zipped up my jacket, pulled on my cap, and applied bug spray. "We must all be insane," I grumbled as I joined my friends in the canoe. "This better be good."

We paddled down the stream and turned left onto a small lake.

"Don't make any noise," Erik whispered.

He clicked on a flashlight and pointed it across the water. A pair of red eyes glowed back at us.

"Gator," Erik said.

Moving the light, he found another pair of eyes.

"How come there aren't more?" I asked softly. "I thought there would be millions."

"There should be," Sharon replied. "Must be because of the poachers."

I heard the sadness in Sharon's voice, and realized that it *was* sad. I wasn't crazy about gators, but if there was anywhere in the world they should be safe, it was here. As Erik's light reflected red from their eyes, the creatures didn't seem so scary anymore. They belonged here. It was easy to imagine, out here where there were hardly any signs of man at all, God creating the Everglades just as he wanted it, crocodiles and alligators and panthers and all, and saying, "That's good." And then man comes along and wants to destroy it just to make a few bucks on alligator purses and boots. What Sharon had said to me over and over suddenly seemed to be true—the gators didn't want to hurt us. They just wanted to be left alone.

Erik shined his light up into the trees. Close by, a pair of green eyes stared at us like marbles. They rose into the air, did a loop-the-loop, and settled back into the tree.

"Owl," whispered Sharon. Cupping her hands to her mouth, she made a deep hooting noise. It sounded funny coming from her. But to my surprise, the owl answered. Sharon hooted again, and the owl replied, then did another loop.

"Neat, huh?" Erik said.

As we paddled on, my paddle touched bottom a few times, and I realized the lake was shallow—in many places just a few inches deep. Some sort of thick moss covered the bottom. My paddle stuck into it, making bubbles and stirring up a thick, mucky swamp smell.

"What's that?" Sharon said, pointing with her paddle.

In the glow of Erik's flashlight we saw a patch of water that seemed to boil. We approached slowly. When we got within a few feet we saw a school of tiny fish swimming and jumping around a long white blob.

"What *is* that?" Erik asked.

"They're eating something," Sharon said. She reached out with her paddle and poked the white thing. It rolled slowly over—a skinned gator!

"Gross!" I said.

"Poachers' work," Sharon said.

"Looks like it's been dead a long time," Erik added, shining his light over it.

"Let's get out of here," Sharon said. "That makes me so mad! Just to make money. . . ."

We headed back to the chickee. Even though we were disturbed by the sight of the dead gator, we were also worn out from the long day's paddle. I fell back asleep as soon as I crawled into my sleeping bag.

Next morning after breakfast we spread the map out.

"Maybe we should head further down the Wilderness Waterway," I said.

"Why?" Erik said. "The poachers must be around here, don't you think?"

"But that gator's been dead a long time," I said. "They might have moved on."

"We could at least look around here for a day or two," Sharon said. She pointed to the map. "This stream we're on leads farther up into the swamp. We might find some sign of the poachers there. What do you think, Eric K.?"

"Let's go for it."

"Erik C.?"

I shrugged. "Okay by me."

Leaving our tents up because we planned to stay another day, we climbed into the canoe and paddled slowly up the stream, which soon narrowed. Gnarled roots scraped the sides of the boat. Branches formed a ceiling overhead like a green tunnel. Butterfly wings winked in the warm air, which smelled of plants and mud and water, and sometimes of flowers.

"I don't think we can go any farther," Sharon said at last, as limbs blocked our way.

"Just a little more," Erik urged. "Push those branches out of the way."

"Watch out for snakes," I warned.

We pulled ourselves under the branches; beyond, the stream widened into a sunny pond.

"Wow!" I said as we drifted onto it and the branches closed behind us. "But how are we going to find our way back?"

"No problem," Erik said. Pulling a red bandanna from his pocket, he tore off a thin strip, which he tied to a limb over our passage. "Now we'll know where to turn in."

We paddled across the pond. It narrowed, and then forked into more streams. Every time it branched off, Erik K. tied a piece of red cloth to mark our way. I felt like a mouse in a maze, following channel after channel, walled in by dense greenery.

As our route twisted and turned, Sharon pointed up ahead. "Look! Somebody else has been here. And they've been using the same kind of markers!"

From a branch hung a strip of red cloth.

10

Erik laughed. "That's our marker."

"No way," Sharon scoffed. "How could it be ours? We've haven't been up there—have we?"

We drifted up to the strip of cloth and Erik pulled it down. "'Fraid so. Look." He held it next to his bandanna. Perfect match. "We've made a big circle."

"Boy, this place is confusing," I said. "I can see how you could get lost."

"Yeah. I'm glad you thought of tying strips of cloth," Sharon told Erik, who tied it back in place.

"Look, here's a channel we haven't tried," Erik said.

We turned into it. We'd only been paddling a few minutes when I spotted something along the bank up ahead. "Hey, what's that?"

"It's grass," Sharon said. Instead of trees crowding the banks, there was tall grass.

"Let's get out and take a look," Erik suggested, grabbing a handful of grass and pulling us to the shore.

"I don't know. Looks kind of snaky to me," I said.

"Oh, come on." As he stepped ashore, he sank to his ankles in mud.

"Yuck!" Sharon said.

But Erik ignored it and disappeared into the grass.

"Don't get lost!" his sister called. She grinned at me. "Sometimes I don't think Erik K. is afraid of anything," she said, sounding more proud than critical. "I'm not sure I want to go in there."

"Hey, come look at these animal tracks!" Erik shouted, and Sharon pulled herself up and stepped out into the mud. It was my turn to grin. If it had to do with animals, Sharon wasn't afraid of much either.

"Let's go look, Eric C.," Sharon said.

Of course, that didn't mean I wasn't afraid. Together, Sharon and I pulled the canoe up into the grass, and I reluctantly followed her, clomping through sticky mud. The grass thinned out, forming a large clearing. Erik stood in the middle of it, studying the ground.

"What are these, sis?" he asked.

Sharon bent down. "Deer tracks. And these are birds, and some kind of heron or crane or something."

"I'll bet this is gator," Erik said, showing us a long, web-toed print.

I looked all around us, to make sure we weren't being ambushed. Then, looking back down, I saw a slithery line in the soft soil. "What's this one?"

"Snake," Sharon said. "See how he crawled?"

"I knew it. I'm out of here." I turned to go back, and I had taken just a few steps when I sank to my knees in the mud. "Hey, give me a hand, you guys! This is quick-mud!"

Erik and Sharon ran over and grabbed my arms. But as they struggled to free me, Sharon lost her balance and plunged face-first into the muck. She tried to push herself up, but the mud was too soft and her arms sank into it up to her shoulders. Finally she pulled her arms out and rolled onto her back. Erik took one look at his sister's face and cracked up. "Hey, nice mudpack, sis!" he choked out.

Wiping mud from her face, she held out her hand. "Make yourself useful, Erik K.—help me up."

As he took her hand, she gave a hard pull. *Plop!* Sharon and I laughed as Erik rose to his knees, covered in sticky goo.

But Erik wasn't an easy one to get the best of. He came up with a handful of mud and an evil grin. "Mud fight!" He threw it straight at his sister. She ducked and the glop landed right in my face.

Soon brown blobs were flying through the air as we pelted one another, laughing wildly. Finally, coated from head to toe, we called a truce and walked back to the canoe.

"I don't know about you guys, but I'm going in," Erik K. said, wading into the water.

"Me too," Sharon said.

"Are you guys crazy? Could be snakes around here, or piranhas or gators." I said.

Ignoring me, they ducked under, dissolving the mud. I watched them for a minute or two, and when nothing gobbled them up I thought, *Aw, what the heck*, and waded out to my waist, then sank to my neck. The cool water soaked my clothes and dissolved the mud in a brown cloud. I held my nose and ducked under, shaking my head to get the mud out of my hair. I came up blowing, then went back under, rubbing my hair with my hand. When I surfaced again, I rubbed all the muck carefully out of my clothes.

When we felt clean we waded out and stood steaming in the sunshine. Then we climbed back into the canoe, pushed off, and paddled back the way we'd come. The blazing sun quickly dried our clothes. We followed our markers back to the chickee and stopped for lunch.

"Well, no more sign of poachers," Sharon said as we ate. "What are we going to do this afternoon?"

"Maybe we should take a nap and let the poachers come to us," I said, yawning.

Erik shook his head. "The fishermen said the Watson Place wasn't far. Why don't we go down there and take a look?"

"The Watson Place?" I protested. "What for? I mean, didn't you hear what the fishermen said? About the legends and everything?"

But Sharon was already studying the map. "Here it is. It's on the Chatham River."

"Don't worry, Eric." Erik K. grinned. "There won't be any ghosts in the daytime."

Soon we were under way, paddling down the stream, which widened as it entered Chatham River.

"The Watson Place should be on the right," Sharon said, the map in her lap. "There's a campsite there."

At last we saw a break in the forest, and a tiny beach where a boat could land. We paddled ashore, climbed out, and walked up the bank to a large, sun-baked clearing.

We all stood silently for a few moments. "Weird," Erik said, wrinkling his nose.

I nodded. "Listen to how quiet it is." Insects hummed eerily in the surrounding forest.

"I'll bet this is where old Mr. Watson lived," Sharon said.

"Look, here's some old bricks," I said. "From his house, maybe."

"What an awful place to live," Sharon said, swatting at a horsefly.

"Wonder how many men he killed right here," I whispered.

"Hush, Eric C.!"

"Hey, footprints," Erik said. He knelt and examined them, then made one of his own right next to them to compare. "These look as fresh as mine!"

11

We paddled swiftly back to camp, all the time watching for strangers.

"I say we radio WSI right now," I said.

"Too soon," Erik said. "That might have been a fisherman's footprints, not a poacher. We should spy on him and find out for sure."

We reached the chickee and climbed up. "Are you kidding?" I said. "What about that dead gator we found last night?"

Sharon nodded. "We should at least tell WSI what we've found. They can tell us what to do next."

Erik dug the radio out of a duffel bag. "Here, Sharon, hand me that map so I can tell them where we are."

As he reached to take the map from his sister, he tried to set the radio on the table beside him. But he was looking at the map, not the radio, and too much of the radio was sticking over the edge of the table when he let go. We watched in horror as it struck the edge of the platform and bounced into the murky water, sinking out of sight.

"Oh no!" Sharon cried.

Without a word Erik peeled his shirt off.

"No, Erik—there's gators here," I said, thinking of the ones we'd seen last night.

"Got to," he said, yanking off his shoes. "Radio's our only way of getting help." He stepped to the edge of the chickee.

"Be careful, Erik!" Sharon called as he dove into the brown water and disappeared. Then we watched, worried, for several seconds as nothing happened. I expected at any minute to see the water boil and turn red with blood.

Instead, Erik punched through the surface, spitting and gasping, holding the radio in his hand. "Got it!"

"All right! Way to go!" Sharon and I shouted, helping him back onto the chickee.

Streaming wet, Erik handed the radio to his sister. "Call them, Sharon, while I dry off."

While he looked for a towel, Sharon pushed the button on the radio. Nothing. She tried it again, then picked the whole thing up and shook it, hard, and pushed the button one more time. Only silence.

"It's not working," she said quietly. "The water must have ruined it."

We took turns trying, but the radio was dead.

"Maybe if we leave it out in the sun to dry, it'll be okay," Erik said. But none of us believed it.

We sat gloomily on the platform. "We might as well go back to Everglades City," I said at last. "If we can't radio WSI, what good can we do?"

Erik sat frowning at his feet. "My fault. If I hadn't dropped the radio. . . ."

Sharon touched his arm. "It could have happened to anybody. We should have brought a back-up, just in case."

He nodded glumly.

"Well?" I said. "Should we go?"

Sharon looked at the sky. "It's already late afternoon. We couldn't get back to Lopez by dark. We'd better stay one more night and leave in the morning."

We were three unhappy campers as we cooked and ate supper. Erik was quiet and sullen, rarely speaking or even looking at Sharon or me.

"It's all right, Erik K.," Sharon said softly.

"Yeah," I added. "We all make mistakes."

But I understood how he felt. We had come all this way for nothing. We'd learned to canoe, flown to Miami, paddled for three days, endured the mosquitoes—and now we would go home defeated.

Except that I'd forgotten who I was dealing with here. Erik suddenly tossed his plate on the table and said, "No! We've got to do something."

66

"What?" I asked. "We tried the radio again and it's no use."

"Then let's paddle down to the Watson Place, tonight, and find out if the poachers are really there. If they are, we can tell WSI as soon as we get out."

"No, Erik K.," Sharon said. "It sounds too dangerous. Maybe this is God's way of telling us we should go home."

"You think every time we have a problem, that means God wants us to quit? No way. God expects us to be tough and take some responsibility."

"But Miss Spice said we weren't supposed to contact the poachers in any way," I said. "Just find them, let WSI know, and get out."

"That's what I'm saying we should do. But first we have to make sure we've found them. So we spy on them tonight."

Sharon and I looked at each other. Neither of us liked the idea much.

"That Watson Place is a long way," I said. "What if we get lost?" I didn't even mention the ghost.

"Look—you guys just stay here, both of you," Erik said. "I dropped the radio. I'll take the risk."

"No," Sharon said. "That would be foolish. I'll come with you. Let Eric C. stay here."

I sighed. "I'll go too."

Erik shook his head. "Someone should stay here, in case there's trouble. That way, somebody knows where we are. You stay, Eric C. Really."

I nodded. Nobody seemed to feel like talking after that, so when the mosquitoes got thick we climbed into our tents to wait for darkness. At last it came.

"Ready, sis?" Erik sounded excited now—anxious, I supposed, to make up for dropping the radio.

"I'm ready," she said. "See you in a little while, Eric C."

I watched as the canoe disappeared in the moonlight. Would they be all right? They could get lost, or the poachers could catch them. Even if everything went according to plan, it might be hours before they returned. I lay back on my sleeping bag to wait.

I must have drifted off. I don't know how long I slept. But something woke me, and I sat up, confused.

Bam! Bam!

Gunshots!

I burst out of the tent. In the moonlight I saw the shape of a canoe moving swiftly my way. I also heard the whine of an engine, and suddenly a bright light appeared, quickly gaining on Erik and Sharon in the canoe—a motorboat!

"Eric! Run! *Run!*" Erik K. shouted.

Run? Where to?

"Jump!" Sharon screamed to me. "Swim to shore! Go for help!"

The light was bearing down on them. Suddenly there was another gunshot. A bullet whistled over my head, and I realized that I was probably visible in the light from the motorboat.

Forgetting that gators lurked underneath, I dove. Cold, dark water covered me. My right hand hit a log. As I grabbed it to push it away, the "log" took off, pulling me behind it.

I was being towed by an alligator!

12

What a choice! Suddenly I knew what people meant by the old saying, "between a rock and a hard place." If I let go of the gator, the bad guys might get me. But if I held on. . . .

I held on—probably not so much because I decided to as just because I was so terrified I couldn't do anything, including letting go. But as the gator pulled me along, I tried to think. The tail didn't feel very big, after all. Maybe this was one of those little guys. Besides, I knew the poachers wanted to hurt me. The bullets proved that. But the gator was probably as scared as I was, and would be happy just to get away.

I rushed along in the cold, dark water, well below the surface, tightly gripping the armored tail. At last

I could hold my breath no longer. I let go and swam to the surface.

I gasped for air and shook my head to clear my eyes. No sign of the gator. Probably hiding in some hole. The chickee, too, was nowhere in sight. In the distance I heard the sound of a motor roaring away, then silence. Swimming to shore, I found myself at the edge of the grassland, and pulled myself up to stand on the soft mud. Silver in the moonlight, the grassy plain stretched away under a starlit sky.

"Sharon! Erik!" I shouted.

No answer. Must have been captured, I hoped. At least that would be better than the alternative.

As I stood there worrying and wondering what to do, mosquitoes pounced. I didn't have a jacket or bug spray to protect me. I had to move!

Heading nowhere in particular, I began to jog. I had to get away from these bloodthirsty insects, and running to stay ahead of them was the only way.

One star seemed brighter than the others. Maybe it was the North Star. I decided to head in that direction. Maybe if I followed it I would get somewhere —anywhere!

The grass stood taller than my head in places. In others, it rose only waist high. Mud sucked at my ankles. Sometimes I wallowed to my knees and had to struggle to get free.

I tried not to think about snakes, gators, or other dangers. Instead, I thought of Sharon and Erik, fleeing for their lives, urging me to run. I couldn't go back—I had to go forward, to find help to send back for them.

If it wasn't already too late. Those poachers, if that's who they were, had been using real bullets—I'd heard them whizzing over my head. Sharon and Erik hadn't answered when I called. I shook my head hard to get rid of the fear that was building inside me and began to pray. I started the Lord's Prayer and hurried to the part that said, "and deliver us from evil."

Please, God, deliver us from evil, I prayed.

He didn't answer out loud, but as I jogged along, dodging through the grass, keeping my eye on the bright North Star, somehow the millions of twinkling stars seemed to speak for him. *If I created all this*, they seemed to say, *do you think I can't protect you and your friends?*

Arriving at a stream, I plunged in up to my chest. "Get away, gators!" I shouted. "Get away, snakes!"

Wading out on the other side, I found the ground a bit firmer. The mosquitoes didn't seem as bad anymore, and a cool breeze had begun to blow.

A deep grunt sounded nearby. Gator! A big one, by the sound of it. I raced faster than ever, even though I was already gasping.

I slowed to a jog again when I thought it was safe. Wait—where was my North Star? Black clouds had begun to cover the sky. The moon vanished as I watched. A blue flash of lightning split the darkness, and thunder shook the ground under my feet.

I remembered the ranger's words: *Watch out for thunderstorms. Lightning is a killer out here.*

Lightning flashed again, followed almost instantly by a terrifying burst of thunder. And here I was in the middle of a grassy plain, with no cover anywhere. Should I keep running, or lie flat?

The next burst convinced me. I fell to my face, lying as flat as possible. *Please, God, deliver us from evil. . . .*

Just then a bomb seemed to explode right next to me. I saw X's inside my skull. I could feel electricity running through my arms and legs, fingers and toes. My body seemed to glow blue. I must have been knocked out, because I dreamed I was floating through space like a lazy comet. It was so quiet and peaceful here.

Slowly I realized the thunderstorm had passed. It echoed in the distance like a bowling alley. I got to my feet, dazed, wondering if I'd been hit. Then I smelled smoke, and noticed the shattered form of a tiny tree. That's what the lightning had struck—just a few yards away!

Boy, was that close!

Thank you, God, for delivering me.

But where to now? I couldn't find the North Star through the clouds. I was tired and sore. My lungs burned and my legs ached.

A light! Off to my right, shining in a clump of trees. Could the poachers have caught up with me?

No, the glow came from a campfire. Had I stumbled across their camp?

On the other hand, it might be someone who could help us. I decided to sneak up and see. If they looked suspicious, I would leave silently. They would never know I was there.

I stopped briefly at the edge of the trees to listen, then moved on carefully, trying not to break branches. This was a good hideout, all right. Too good, in fact. No one in his right mind would come to a place like this.

What if it was a madman, a crazy swamp hermit? Or an escaped convict? Or even—I shuddered—the ghost of Mr. Watson?

I started to sneak away, but my aching legs stopped me. I needed to rest. And after all, what if this was, say, a Scoutmaster, or park ranger? Crouching behind a screen of bushes, I peered at the fire.

No one was there, though it flickered brightly. A long, thin piece of meat was roasting over the flames. Oh, gross—it was snake! Anybody crazy enough to camp out here and cook snake was too crazy for me. I began to back away.

Suddenly a strong hand grabbed the back of my shirt and yanked me to my feet. Before I could move, the cold blade of a knife pressed against my throat.

"Start talking," said a deep voice. "Who are you, and what do you want?"

13

The man dragged me out into the firelight, peered into my face—and let go of my collar in surprise. "You're just a kid!" He sheathed his knife.

I tried to speak but could only cough.

"Oh, a Scout," he said, eyeing my uniform. "Must be getting a merit badge, huh? Sit down."

I sank onto a log and the man sat across from me. He had longish black hair and brown skin. He wore a denim shirt, blue jeans, and high, black rubber boots. He looked like an Indian, and I remembered reading in school about an Indian tribe that lived in the Everglades.

"Are you a Seminole?"

He shook his head. "No such thing as Seminoles."

"Sure there are—I read about them in social studies. They had that famous chief, Osceola."

The man nodded. "Osceola was a great chief. Me, I'm no chief. Just Billy Smith. Who are you?"

"Eric Sterling, sir. Friends call me Eric C."

He stuck his hand out and we shook. He had a grip that could hold a gator's mouth shut. "Sorry about the knife, Eric C. You got to be careful these days. When you come up on a campfire at night, you'd best announce yourself loud and clear, so people know you're friendly."

"I understand," I said, flexing my fingers.

He checked his snake meat and shifted it closer to the fire, then settled back onto his log and stared off into the night. I was just about to decide that he matched the stereotype of the silent red man when he grinned and looked back at me. "Seminoles." He shook his head. "You're a Scout. You study about Indians. You want to hear about the real Indians of the Everglades?"

"Sure."

"When the white man landed, the Calusa Indians ruled this country. All of south Florida, from Tampa to Key West, was Calusa land. But guns, whiskey, and disease wiped them out. Then, since the land was empty, other tribes moved in, forced by the white man. All these different groups became known as Seminoles, which means outsiders. So the Seminoles aren't a true tribe, but a collection of others."

Slightly confused, I asked, "So what are you?"

His back straightened slightly. "The history books say there aren't any more Calusas, but that's not true. My grandfather was a Calusa. A small group of them moved to Cuba when he was a boy. When he grew up, he came back to Florida. Now he's dead and my parents are dead." He paused for a second or two and looked straight into my eyes, proud. "I am Red Thunder, the last of the Calusas."

"Wow!"

But Red Thunder seemed sad as well as proud. Sighing, he pulled his knife from its sheath and poked the roasting snake. "Supper's ready."

Uh-oh. I watched as he lay it on some leaves. Pulling off a strip of meat, he handed it to me. I didn't dare refuse.

"Eat!" he commanded, tossing a chunk into his own mouth.

I put a piece of roasted snake into my mouth and chewed slowly. It tasted like turkey breast a week after Thanksgiving, dry and tough but not bad.

"Better get used to this kind of food if you're going to learn to live off the land," Red Thunder said. "Plenty of snakes out here."

"Yes, sir."

When we finished eating, he offered me a drink from his canteen. "Do you live out here?" I asked.

He shook his head. "I work at a cigar factory in Tampa. I just come here sometimes to get back to the land. Here, have a cigar." He pulled two from his shirt pocket and tossed one to me. "Rolled them myself," he said proudly.

I stared at the thick roll of brown tobacco.

"Something wrong with it?" he asked with a frown.

I stuck one end into my mouth. The Indian chuckled, yanked it out, bit the tip off, and shoved it between my lips. Then he took a burning stick from the campfire and held it to the end of my cigar.

"Puff!" he ordered. "That's it."

Strong-tasting smoke filled my mouth and nose. I coughed violently. Red Thunder patted my back with a laugh.

"Never smoked a cigar before, huh?" he asked, lighting his own.

"No, sir."

"Smoked my first when I was six."

After a few more puffs, I decided it wasn't so bad. I grinned. If my parents could see me now, they'd throw a fit. Somehow that made it taste even better. Clouds of smoke rose around my head, mixing with smoke from the campfire.

"Nothing like a good cigar after a meal," Red Thunder said.

"You bet!"

I gazed happily into the flames. *Yessir, nothing like a good cigar after a meal,* I thought.

By the time my cigar was about a third gone, I began to feel a little dizzy. I puffed on for a few more minutes and felt even sicker. It was the tobacco, of course. But I wouldn't give up.

"Yes, sir, the Everglades is fine country," he was saying. "Wild and untamed. Just wish it would stay that way." He shook his head sadly. "But all this development is killing it—poachers, farming, subdivisions. Miami's growing every day."

I couldn't make any sense out of his words, and finally I stopped hearing them as waves of nausea swept through me.

Dropping my cigar, I slid to the ground and lay on my side, wishing the world would stop spinning.

"Sleepy?" Red Thunder said. "Me too." He unrolled a sleeping bag, removed his boots, and climbed in. "Good night, kid."

But the night didn't feel so good to me. Is it possible, I wondered, to die from an overdose of tobacco?

14

When I finally fell asleep, I dreamed I was in a lifeboat. Tossing up and down in the ocean made me seasick. I woke late the next morning with a stale taste in my mouth. Staggering to my feet, still woozy, I took a deep drink from the canteen.

"Morning," Red Thunder said, roasting a pair of fish over the campfire.

"Good morning."

"Found these fish on my droplines this morning. Know how to set a dropline, kid?"

"No, sir."

He looked up, surprised. "A Scout who doesn't know how to set a dropline?"

I decided to change the subject quickly. "Can you tell me where the nearest road is?"

He pointed across the grassland. "See that line of trees way over there? On the other side is a highway. That where you're headed?"

"Yes, sir."

"Well, have some breakfast first."

We divided up the fish, which tasted better than snake. It made me feel stronger and less woozy. As I gobbled every last morsel, I wondered—should I tell him about Erik K. and Sharon? Maybe he could help rescue them. But what did I know about him? Not much. And why had he been so worried about me last night that he'd pulled a knife? How did I know he wasn't a poacher himself? No, my best bet was to contact WSI—quickly. I stood. "Well, Mr. Thunder, guess I'll be on my way."

He looked up and nodded, then began to fish around in his shirt pocket. "Before you go, I want to give you something." Oh no, not another cigar! But he pulled out a small stone and tossed it to me.

"An arrowhead!"

He nodded. "Belonged to my grandpa. Maybe it will bring you luck."

"Thanks, Mr. Thunder."

"You may need it."

I left the little grove of trees. Wading a stream, I saw a small canoe tied to a tree. So that's how Red Thunder got here.

The waist-deep grass and wet ground made for slow going. Biting flies pestered me, and I sometimes slipped, falling to my knees in the muck. Sweat poured down my skin. Boy, could I use another drink from Red Thunder's canteen!

At last I reached the trees, and found the mud there even deeper. I sank to my knees in places. I could hear traffic up ahead, and soon I saw cars whisking by on a raised highway. Stumbling out of the forest, I climbed the bank to the pavement.

Whoosh! An 18-wheeler sped past. Down the road to my left I noticed a small convenience store. As I walked, an endless stream of cars and trucks roared past me. No wonder vehicles killed so many panthers!

By the time I reached the store, I thought I was going to die of thirst. The first thing I planned to do was buy a big jug of ice-cold orange juice. Then I would phone WSI for help.

Inside, a pretty, young black woman sat behind the counter reading a magazine. "Hello," she said, looking up with a smile.

"Hi." My voice cracked with thirst. I got a bottle of juice from a cooler, set it on the counter, and reached for my wallet.

It was gone! It must have fallen out of my pocket when I dove into the swamp.

Tears filled my eyes. I was so parched I could almost taste that cold, sweet juice. Now I'd have to do without.

"What's the matter, sugar?" the woman asked. Then, realizing my problem, she opened the container and handed it to me with a smile. "On the house."

"Wow! Thanks." Grabbing it, I drank deeply. Nothing ever tasted so good.

"What's your name, anyway?" she asked when I had finished.

"Eric Sterling."

She nodded. "I thought so."

"What do you mean?"

She took a quick look around the store to make sure we were alone. Then she reached into her purse and pulled out a wallet. Flipping it open, she showed me a badge. "Delia Simmons. Special agent, WSI."

I stared at her, amazed. Then I remembered Miss Spice saying WSI had agents on stand-by in the area.

"Come on," Delia said. "Let's get you cleaned up."

Hanging a "closed" sign on the door, Delia led me out back to a small house. She waved me into the bathroom and said, "You get a nice hot bath. Hand me those clothes out and I'll throw them in the washer."

Soon I was soaking in a tub full of hot water. *Aaaah!* I knew it would take her a while to wash my clothes, so I settled in for a long one, adding more hot water every now and then. I was finished and toweling myself off when she handed my clothes in, clean and dry. She had even found me a new belt to replace the soggy one I'd been wearing.

As soon as I stepped out I smelled home cooking.

"Thought you might be hungry," Delia said. "After you eat, you can tell me your story."

I sat down to a plate loaded with fried catfish, hush puppies, cole slaw, and mashed potatoes, with plenty of iced tea on the side. Boy! It sure beat snake. Finally I sat back, satisfied.

"Now," said Delia, sipping a cup of coffee. "I want to hear all about it."

I told her everything, about our camp at Sweet-water, the gunmen chasing Erik K. and Sharon, and me fleeing for my life.

Delia nodded grimly. "Sounds like poachers, all right. If they've captured your friends, they probably know we're after them. We need to get out there right away."

She unrolled a map of the Everglades. "Let's see, you were at Sweetwater . . . Your friends were captured here . . . Hey! I'll bet those poachers are hiding out at the Watson Place!"

I remembered the fresh footprints, and told her about them. "But it seems like there would have been more signs of people."

"You just went to the first clearing," Delia told me. "There's another one back in the woods. You may have been right near them and didn't know it."

Scary thought.

"Come on. Let's take my boat. Your friends could be in danger."

Soon we were whizzing into the swamp in a motorboat.

"This is Turner River," Delia shouted over the noise of the engine. "I grew up around here, near Everglades City."

"How did you get into WSI?" I shouted back.

"I was helping my daddy fish in the Gulf. He's a commercial fisherman. One day a WSI agent came to our house and asked me to join. He said they wanted someone who knew a lot about the swamp."

She veered down a channel to the left. Soon I recognized the markers for the Wilderness Waterway. Amazing how fast we went in this motorboat, compared to the canoe.

"The Watson Place is a perfect spot for poachers," Delia called. "It's not far from the Gulf. That way a yacht can come in, collect the hides, and go back to sea before anybody catches them." She slowed the boat. "Here's Chatham River. Down here to the right is the Watson Place."

Suddenly she gunned the motor, steering the boat fast down the river.

"Aren't you afraid they'll hear us?" I said.

But Delia didn't look at me. "Delia?" I said, beginning to get a funny feeling about this. Soon I saw the little beach at the Watson Place. Delia motored right to it.

"Get out," she said as we nudged up to the beach.

"Are you crazy? Delia—"

Just then two men with shotguns walked out of the trees. One was a big man wearing dirty, blue overalls, the other much smaller in a green jumpsuit. "What took you so long, Delia?" asked the short man with a grin.

She shrugged. "He's yours now, Jake. You've got

all three. You and Hubert shouldn't have any more trouble with WSI."

The taller man pointed his shotgun at me and motioned me onto the beach. I stepped out of the boat, then stared at Delia in shock.

But she wouldn't look back, and without a word she cranked the engine and roared away. Flanked by the two men, I walked across the clearing. Our canoe and a motorboat lay half-hidden in the weeds; that meant that Erik and Sharon were okay. A path led through the woods to another meadow, where two tents stood. I sniffed a funny, sweetish, musky smell that made me wrinkle my nose. Then I saw, in the shade of a tree, a long folding table with a dead gator, six feet long, lying on its back. A slit ran down its belly, and two bloody skinning knives lay beside it. Yellowjackets swarmed around the table.

We stopped in front of a tent. Jake frisked me, then opened a padlock that held the zippers shut. "Get in that tent, punk." He pushed me inside and locked it behind me.

As I expected, Erik K. and Sharon were in the tent. Despite everything, I was so happy to see them alive and well that I reached out and touched them both.

"What happened?" Erik asked me. "How'd they catch you?"

I scowled. "I've been double-crossed by a WSI agent!"

15

"How did you two get captured?" I asked, after telling them my story.

"We were paddling down to the Watson Place when we saw a light," Erik said. We were sitting cross-legged, knee to knee in the small tent. "We turned to get away, but the light shone right on us."

"A voice shouted for us to halt," Sharon added. "We thought maybe if we paddled fast we could hide. But they cranked a motor and started shooting."

"We got close enough to Sweetwater to warn you," Erik continued. "But after you jumped, the men caught up with us. They brought us here and put us in this tent."

"We learned a lot, though, just by listening to them talking," Sharon said. "There are two of them, and they've got a big shipment of hides here. A yacht is supposed to come in sometime tonight and pick up the skins."

"If only I hadn't dropped that radio!" Erik said. "These guys would have been in jail by now, and we'd be on our way back home."

He looked pretty sad, but he couldn't have felt any worse than I did. I still couldn't believe Delia was one of them. "What do you think they'll do with us?" I whispered.

Erik shrugged and then punched the air angrily. "I hate being stuck here! I just wish there were some way to get out. We could cut our way out, but those guys took my pocket knife. And the zipper's got a lock on it."

"Yeah," I said. "They frisked me too." Then I remembered something. Reaching into my pocket, I pulled out the flat arrowhead.

"Wow!" Erik said. "Where'd you get that?"

"Red Thunder, the Indian, gave it to me for good luck."

"Looks like it'll bring us good luck, all right," Erik said. "Soon as it gets dark we can cut this tent open and escape."

"But where can we go?" I asked.

"I remember from the map the best way to get back," Sharon said. "We just paddle right down this river and come out to the Gulf. Then we turn right and follow the coast all the way back to the ranger station."

"At night?" I asked doubtfully.

"Come on, there'll be plenty of moonlight," Erik said. "We can do it!"

"Besides," Sharon said, "would you rather take your chances on the water—or with these crooks?"

At about sundown the men fed us bowls of greasy canned chili and a canteen of water. Then, when it got dark, we heard them roar away into the swamp in their motorboat.

"Probably going to hunt more gators," Sharon said angrily.

"Come on," Erik said. "Now's our chance!"

With the arrowhead I sliced a long slit in the tent. Hungry mosquitoes swarmed around us as we climbed out, and we slapped at them as we raced to our canoe, pulled on our life vests, and slid the boat into the water. Praying the poachers wouldn't come back for some reason and find us, we paddled feverishly down the river. Soon we felt a stiff breeze that smelled of seaweed.

"Look! The Gulf!" Erik said, pointing to a vast sheet of moon-crinkled water.

"Boy, the wind's strong out here!" Sharon said as we paddled into the waves. Spray flew into our faces, cold and salty-tasting, like dill pickle juice. Water sloshed over the sides, wetting our clothes. Farther out in the Gulf we saw whitecaps.

"Maybe we should go back," I said. "We could try to follow the Wilderness Waterway or something."

"No, the poachers might find us!" Erik argued.

As we turned right along the coast, the sea battered us so that our canoe pitched up and down, back and forth, and we could barely control it.

"We shouldn't turn sideways!" I shouted, remembering our canoe lessons. "Angle into the waves!"

Working together, we kept the dark, tree-lined shore to our right, the open Gulf to our left.

"Must be a storm blowing up," Sharon said.

"Think we should land until it passes?" I said.

"Land where?" Erik said. "It's all mud and—what do you call those trees with all the roots?"

"Mangroves," Sharon said.

A big wave hit us, dumping several inches of water in the boat and totally soaking us.

"I'm getting scared," Sharon said.

"We're doing okay," Erik said. "Just keep angling into the waves!"

Lightning splintered over the Gulf. I flinched, recalling the bolt that had almost hit me. Black clouds covered the sky, leaving us in total darkness except for the flashes.

"We've got to land!" Sharon said, shouting to be heard over the wind. "We can't keep on like this—we'll capsize!"

"You're right!" Erik shouted. "Let's head back to shore, try to find a beach—anything would be better than this!" If even Erik was willing to call it quits, I knew we were in real danger.

We·turned the boat toward the coast. But as we did, it swung sideways into the waves—at just the wrong time.

"Look out!" I yelled.

A wall of water hit us like a speeding car. In a split second the canoe was upside down, and the three of us were thrashing in an angry sea!

16

"Is everybody okay?" Erik shouted. "Sharon? Eric? Where are you?"

"I'm okay!" Sharon called.

"Me too!" I said.

"Everybody hold onto the boat!"

I could barely make out the shapes of my friends in the darkness. We clung to the bottom of the upturned boat, which wallowed in the water.

"What are we going to do, Erik K.?" Sharon said.

"I don't know. Let me think."

"Maybe we should try to swim for shore," I suggested.

"No!" Erik said. "We can't even *see* it. Maybe the moon will come back out soon."

The waves tossed us up and down. Though we had on life vests, I was scared. I thought about sharks, and about drifting far out to sea.

Sharon screamed. "Something just brushed my leg!"

Erik dove under. We heard bumping noises under the canoe. What was he doing, fighting a shark? Then he surfaced. "It's all right. It was just this paddle. It was trapped under the boat. Look, we've got to stay calm."

"You're right," Sharon said. "We've got to have faith."

I snorted. "Yeah, like I had faith in Delia."

"I mean faith in God," she said.

"Maybe," I muttered. "I'm just finding it a little tough to have faith in anything or anyone right now. I mean, if God's taking care of us, why are we in this mess? Why didn't he—*hey!*"

Something bumped my leg—something big. I tried to yell again, to tell the others to watch out, but visions of JAWS filled my mind and all I could do was croak.

"What is it, Eric?" Erik K. shouted.

And in the couple of seconds it took for me to find my voice and try to answer, the clouds parted, the moon shone through, and I found myself staring at the strangest thing I'd ever seen.

A few feet away, a huge animal floated calmly in the water. It had a fat nose and two gentle, dark eyes.

"Hey!" Sharon shouted. "A sea cow!"

The creature made a deep, grunting noise, and a much smaller head appeared next to it.

"A baby!" Sharon said. We all laughed at the wide little eyes blinking curiously at us.

The sea cow and her child circled us slowly, staying several feet away. Then the large one approached Sharon.

"Be careful," Erik said.

"Don't be silly. They're very gentle." She reached out and stroked the mother, which closed its eyes with a happy groan. The baby, eager to be petted, pushed its parent aside and stuck its own head under Sharon's hand. "Sweet little thing," Sharon cooed. "I wish you could come home with me."

The mother dove and rubbed against the canoe.

"Hey, maybe she's trying to turn the canoe over," Erik K. said.

"She's just scratching her back," Sharon said.

Just then the mama sea cow surfaced with a sharp barking noise. The baby disappeared underwater, followed by its mother.

"What happened?" I asked.

"Something scared them," Sharon said.

Then, over the roar of the waves, we heard the distant sound of an approaching motor.

"Uh-oh," Erik said.

Far out in the Gulf we saw the lights of a boat, heading straight for the mouth of the Chatham River.

"Poachers!" I said.

"Would the poachers have their lights on?" Sharon wondered aloud.

"They might have to, in this storm," Erik said.

"What if it's the Coast Guard?" Sharon suggested. "They could rescue us."

"We can't take that chance," Erik said.

A searchlight beam from the boat swept across the water.

"Probably looking for the mouth of the river," Erik said. "Hey, the light's coming our way. Everybody duck!"

I took a deep breath and went under. All I could hear were the sounds of water sloshing against the boat. Finally I could hold my breath no longer, and I came up—right into the blinding glare of the searchlight!

Sharon blinked at me, her hair plastered to her head. "They must have seen the canoe."

Erik popped up, gasping.

"We're caught," I said as the motor grew louder and the vessel plowed toward us.

"Let's hope it's the Coast Guard," Sharon said, her voice shaking from the cold.

"What if it's the poachers?" I said. "I don't want to be caught again."

"Maybe we should swim for shore," Erik said. "We can see better now."

"We'd never make it," Sharon said. "That boat would catch us before we even got close."

The boat approached rapidly, its searchlight blinding us. As it pulled alongside, a man shouted, "Are you kids okay?"

"See?" Sharon whispered. "I told you it was the Coast Guard."

The man, who wore a captain's hat, slid a ladder over the side. "Come on up. Be careful. Watch your step."

We climbed out of the water and stood dripping wet on deck. With the searchlight out of our eyes, we could see now that it was a large yacht, clean and well cared for. The captain spoke into a radio. "This is *Sea Predator* calling base camp, do you read me?"

The radio crackled. "Go ahead, *Sea Predator*."

"We found the three kids and we're coming in."

"Roger, over."

I began to relax. Maybe Sharon was right about having faith.

The captain clicked off the radio and stared at us with a cold grin. "You kids escaped once, but you won't get away again!"

17

The captain pushed us into the boat's cabin and closed the wooden door behind us. We heard him bolt it shut.

We were trapped. There were no windows and only one door, and it was locked. It was pitch dark in here, and cramped. Still dripping wet, uncomfortable, and cold, we sat on bunks and listened as the yacht motored across the choppy water. When the waves stopped slapping the boat we knew we had entered Chatham River.

"I guess we should have tried to swim for shore," Sharon said.

"Nah—you were right, we'd never have made it," Erik said sadly. "Let's face it, we're caught. And we failed in our mission."

"Doesn't take a genius to figure out that we're headed back to the Watson Place, and when we get there they'll load all the alligator hides onto this boat," I said. "But then what? Where will they go? And what'll they do with us?"

"My guess is they'll go around to Miami, or maybe cut straight across to Central America," Sharon said.

"And they'll probably keep us as hostages," Erik added.

"Hostages? In *Central America*?" I groaned. "We'll never escape!"

"Or maybe they'll just tie rocks to us and throw us over the side," Erik said gloomily.

"Oh, Erik K., hush!" said his sister. "You'll get us so depressed we won't be able to think. We've got to think positive."

"Sorry, Sharon, but I'm having a little trouble coming up with any positive thoughts at the moment," I said sarcastically.

"Don't you see?" Sharon said. "Every time we've gotten into trouble, God has helped us."

"Are you *crazy*?" I scoffed.

"Uh, Sharon," Erik said. "We're not exactly out of trouble."

"Think about it," she said. "When they were shooting at us, none of us was hurt. When they put us in the tent, Eric C. showed up with an arrowhead. When something brushed against us in the water, it turned out to be a sea cow. Now we're in trouble again—and God will show us a way out of here, too."

I could hear Erik squirming around as if he were getting agitated. "Look, I believe in God, too," he said. "But I think we'd be stupid to just sit around waiting for God to get us out of this mess, you know?"

"I'm not saying we should just sit around," Sharon answered quietly. "On the other hand, it worked okay for Daniel, when he was in the lions' den."

I shook my head. "I don't feel like Daniel right now. Maybe we're doomed. Maybe there is no way out."

The cabin grew quiet. I wondered what my friends were thinking. I had the feeling Sharon was praying quietly.

The motor stopped and the boat bumped the shore. We heard voices.

"Must be the Watson Place," I whispered.

"Listen. They're going ashore," Erik said.

We heard footsteps cross a gangplank, and the voices faded. Erik jumped up and tried the door knob. "Locked up tight." He tried his shoulder against it a couple of times, without luck.

In a few minutes we heard footsteps again, followed by grunts and the sound of heavy bundles being dropped.

"They're loading the gator hides on board," Sharon whispered. Soon the men left again.

"Got to be a way out of here," Erik muttered. I could hear him feeling the wall with his hands.

"Too bad we can't kick the door down," I said.

There was a moment of silence, and then Erik laughed. "Thanks, Eric. Where's my head, man? I break boards all the time in karate class. Stand back, everybody."

"Be careful, Erik K.," Sharon cautioned. "It might be too hard."

"Don't you remember that time I broke three boards in the tournament?" he reminded his sister. "This door can't be any thicker than that. Here goes."

With a grunt he slammed the bottom of his foot against the door. It made a cracking noise but didn't give. "Man!" he said. "Must be plywood."

"What difference would that make?" I asked.

"Plywood is several sheets of wood turned cross-ways to each other. It's almost impossible to break."

The boat rocked as he kicked the door again. It still didn't budge.

"Erik K., you're going to hurt yourself," Sharon said. "Let's think of something else."

"One more time."

"Better hurry. They'll be back any second," I urged. *Bam!*

"Hey, I'm stuck!" he said. His foot had gone all the way through the door.

"All right!" Sharon and I shouted as we helped him pull his leg back through the ragged hole.

"You deserve a trophy for that, for sure," I said as he reached through the hole and unbolted the door. Swinging it open, he hurried on deck in the moonlight, followed by Sharon and me.

"Hurry," Erik whispered, "before they get back."

"But we don't have a boat," I whispered back.

"Then we'll just have to go on foot. Come on."

As he led the way down the gangplank we saw flashlights coming through the woods. "This way," Erik whispered, and ducked into the woods to our left.

The small trees grew close together, their roots criss-crossing the muddy ground. I felt like a bug in a spider web as we clambered, stumbled, and crawled.

Soon we heard shouts behind us—the men must have discovered our escape.

"It's okay. They'll never find us in here," Erik said. "Look, the woods are opening up some."

With the trees farther apart and the ground clearer, we could move swiftly. Mosquitoes buzzed around us, but at least the poachers were far behind. When we could no longer hear them, we stopped to catch our breaths.

"Wonder where we are," I said.

"I'll bet this is part of Mr. Watson's old farm," Sharon said.

"Watson!" In the faint moonlight, with violent criminals on my trail, the thought of the old murderer was so spooky I wanted to run. "Come on, let's get out of here."

I had only run a few steps when I tripped on something and crashed to the ground. When I tried to get up, my foot was stuck tight. I pulled—what was that? An eerie moan. The hair stood up on the back of my neck as I looked toward the sound and saw a light bobbing slowly through the trees.

"It's the ghost of Mr. Watson!" I cried. I pulled and pulled, but whatever had my foot wouldn't let go. "Help me! I'm trapped!"

18

"What's going on here?" a man's voice asked.

"Red Thunder!" I shouted happily. I fell back onto the ground and let the fear and tension drain away. "Boy, am I glad to see you. Could you give me a hand here—I'm caught."

"You sure are," he said, shining his flashlight on me. "You're tangled in some old nylon fishing line." He knelt to unravel it. "This stuff is a real menace. Some fishermen are too lazy to take their old line home, and animals get trapped just like you are." Freeing my foot, he helped me up.

"Thanks. But what was that moaning sound?"

"That?" He laughed, then cupped his hand to his mouth and made the noise. "Don't you recognize a screech owl call?"

"Erik, Sharon, this is Red Thunder," I told my friends, who approached cautiously.

"Glad to meet you," the Indian said. "Both named Eric, huh?"

We laughed. "Yes, sir. It's a long story—we'll tell you some time."

"What are you kids doing out here in the middle of the night?"

"That's a long story, too, Mr. Thunder," I said.

"Well, come on back to camp and tell me all about it."

We followed him onto a hill overlooking the Gulf of Mexico. With the storm past, the moon shone across the water.

"How do you like my camping spot?" Red Thunder asked.

"Great!" Erik said. "No mosquitoes!"

"Well, hardly any," Sharon said, slapping her neck.

As he poked up the campfire, Red Thunder smiled. "The breeze from the Gulf keeps them off. If you're going to travel in the swamp, you have to know how to pick a good campsite. This place has been used by Indians for centuries."

"It's not even muddy here," Sharon said, kicking at the ground.

"It's a shell mound," he explained. "The Calusa Indians caught oysters in the Gulf and threw the shells into a pile. Over the years it became a hill—a good spot to camp, don't you think?"

"And what a view," Sharon said, stepping to the edge of the hill.

Standing beside her, I felt the warm night breeze tug at my hair. She was right, it was beautiful. But the miles of empty space—moonlight, stars, water—made me ache inside for some reason. Homesickness?

"You kids like fish?" Red Thunder asked, and I turned back to the firelight.

"You bet!" Erik K. said, spotting half a dozen grilling over the fire.

"I think these are ready. Here, sit down and eat. Two for each of you."

"What about you?" Sharon asked.

"I already ate."

We sat cross-legged on the shells and chowed down. The fish had a chewy skin that tasted of charcoal and lots of tender white meat. When we finished, we passed around the canteen for long swigs.

"Now," Red Thunder said. "Tell me what you're really doing out here—and don't pretend you're working on merit badges." I looked up to see if he was angry, but there was a twinkle in his eye.

We told him the whole story. When we got to the part about the poachers loading alligator skins onto the yacht, Red Thunder scowled.

"You see?" he said. "Like I was telling you, Eric— that's what's happening to the Everglades! People are killing it. When I was a boy there were thousands of gators here." He stood up. "Well, we'll just stop these poachers."

We looked at him. "But how?" I asked.

"The Calusa way." The look in his eyes sent a chill down my spine. I noticed the big hunting knife on his hip. "Which one of you is the strongest paddler?"

"Erik K.," Sharon and I replied.

"My canoe's at the bottom of this hill, on the Gulf side," he told Erik, pointing. "You know the way back to the Watson Place?"

"Sure," Erik answered. "Well—maybe."

"I do," Sharon said. "I remember it from the map."

Red Thunder nodded and pointed his finger at Sharon and then at Erik. "You two take the canoe around to the Watson Place. Pull up under some bushes and wait, in case we need your help. Eric C., you come with me."

"Okay, but what's the plan?" I said. "What—"

Red Thunder was already walking away.

"See you guys later," I said over my shoulder as I hurried after him.

The Indian clicked on his flashlight, and I followed its bobbing beam. He stopped at a small creek and shined his light in the water.

"Hold this light," he commanded.

I took it as he knelt to scoop a handful of white mud from the bottom. He began to smear it on his face.

"What's that for?" I asked.

"War paint," he grunted.

Soon his face was solid white. He took the flashlight from me, and we walked on. As we neared the

Watson Place, he cut the light off. We sneaked up to the path near the boat and crouched behind some brush. From the meadow came the sound of men talking.

"Here, help me get this tent down, Hubert." I recognized Jake's voice.

"Hurry up. If those kids find help, we won't have much time," the captain said.

Jake snorted. "They won't get far. Buncha green-horns."

"Snakes'll get 'em, sure," Hubert said.

"Take this light," Red Thunder whispered. "Run down to the boat and see if their guns are there. If they are, drop them overboard. I'll whistle if I hear them coming."

"But they'll catch me!"

"Not if you hurry. Now go!" He pushed me toward the path.

I dashed down the bank, across the gangplank and onto the yacht. Switching on the flashlight and crouching low, I quickly checked the decks. No guns. Then I poked the light into the cabin. There they were, three of them lying on a bunk! I carried them quickly outside and slid them into the dark water, where they vanished with barely a splash. I was about to race back to Red Thunder when I heard a low whistle.

Flashlights appeared on the trail. I was trapped!

19

Panicked, I turned off my light and ducked into the cabin, crouching in the darkness. The men's footsteps sounded on the wooden plank, and the boat rocked slightly. If they looked in here, I was dead meat!

"We got a fortune in hides here," Jake grunted, dropping a bundle of hides with a thud.

"Yeah, but that just about cleans out this area," the captain said. "We'll have to move on down the Waterway."

"Suits me," Hubert said. "This place gives me the creeps anyway. All that talk about Old Watson's ghost—"

The captain snorted. "Don't believe that nonsense."

"Easy for you to say," Jake replied. "You didn't have to stay here night after night. I'm telling you, there's something about this place."

"And that's exactly why it was a good camp," said the captain. "No one bothered you here, no one came poking around. The legend keeps them away."

"I reckon that's true," Hubert said. "Still, good thing we got that WSI gal on our side."

"Yeah—wasn't for Delia, they might've caught us by now," Jake agreed.

We definitely would have, I thought, feeling hurt and betrayed all over again. Delia. I shook my head. How could a person seem so kind and be so deceitful?

"What else is there?" the captain asked.

"The table. A duffel bag. I don't know what else," Jake replied.

"Well, come on. We can't afford to leave any evidence, anything they might trace to us. Double-check the whole area."

The men left the boat. As soon as their flashlights disappeared into the trees, I dashed to shore.

"What happened?" Red Thunder asked.

"I hid in the cabin. They'd have caught me if they looked in there."

"You did well. Now I have one other job."

"Another one!"

"I want you to go down and untie the yacht. Let it drift downstream."

"What'll you do?"

112

"There's no time. Go!"

I sprinted back to the boat, quickly found where the men had knotted a thick rope to a leaning tree, and struggled to untie it. A whistle sounded! Too soon—the men were coming back and the yacht was still tied up! Then the whistle sounded again, and I realized that it was a real bird, not Red Thunder. Calming myself, I worked steadily to untie the knot. At last the rope dropped to the ground—but the big boat didn't move in the still river.

Lifting the end of the heavy gangplank, I pushed it back onto the yacht. Then I leaned against the hull and gave a hard shove. To my surprise, the yacht glided easily out onto the river in the moonlight.

Then I noticed the small motorboat beside it. Red Thunder hadn't mentioned it—what was his plan? Would he want this boat or not? I wished he'd told me what he was up to. Not sure whether I was doing the right thing or not, I pushed it away too. Soon both boats were drifting downstream.

At that instant I heard a shout.

"It's the ghost!" Hubert bellowed.

"Run, it's old Watson!" Jake cried.

Three flashlight beams bobbed crazily through the forest as the three men rushed toward me, trying to run but bouncing off trees and tripping over bushes in their fright. I ducked behind a tree. Then I saw what frightened them: Behind them, looming out of the forest, an eerie white face floated in the darkness.

It grinned like an evil jack-o-lantern, and a terrifying howl came from its mouth. I pressed myself against the tree trunk, trembling. This was worse than Jason and Freddy Krueger rolled into one.

"The boats are gone!" the captain shouted.

"Where are the guns?"

"We're trapped!"

"Jump in!"

There were three quick splashes as the men hit the river head-first and began swimming like crazy straight out away from the shore. Just then a bright spotlight came on from further out in the river, pinning the men like scared rabbits.

"Don't move!" a woman's voice commanded.

"Delia!" Jake said shakily. "That you?"

"Yes, it's me. Stay where you are."

The moan sounded again, and we all glanced back to see the ghost moving slowly closer. Delia pointed her spotlight at it—Red Thunder! He was holding his flashlight under his chin aimed straight up, turning his painted face into a horrible mask.

So he was the "ghost!" I almost laughed.

Then I realized that Delia probably had a gun, and might be taking aim at him at this instant.

"Run, Red Thunder!" I yelled. "She's on their side!"

20

"No!" Sharon's voice sounded nearby. "She's on our side, Eric C. Really!"

"That's right," Erik K. said as their canoe emerged from the shadows and nudged the riverbank near me.

"All right, you three," Delia told the poachers, who were treading water, sticking close to each other. "I've got a .357 magnum aimed right at you, so do what I say. Swim back to shore, and then stand there at the water's edge." They splashed slowly toward shore.

She cranked a motor, puttered behind them up to the bank, then climbed out and handcuffed the men expertly. "On your knees, and no tricks."

Grumbling, the men obeyed.

"Way to go, Mr. Thunder!" Sharon said as she and Erik jumped ashore.

"I thought you were going to scalp them!" Erik said.

The Indian grinned. "Scalping is not the Calusa way. But scaring is. You see, the legend of a ghost was here long before Mr. Watson. When the first white men came, my people created the 'ghost' to keep them away from our hunting and fishing grounds. After Mr. Watson was killed, the story grew, and people started calling it the ghost of Mr. Watson."

"So there never was a ghost?" Erik said.

Red Thunder put his finger to his lips. "Don't tell. I *like* people to think there's a ghost back here."

Delia smiled and extended her hand. "Mr. Thunder, I'm Delia Simmons, Wildlife Special Investigations." They shook hands. "Thanks to you and these three young agents, we have just caught some of the most dangerous and damaging poachers in the Everglades."

He shrugged. "I just wanted to stop them from destroying the gators." He pointed at me. "If Eric C. here hadn't done his part, they'd have had guns in their hands just now, and we'd have really had problems."

Delia turned to me. "Hello, Eric C.," she said softly. She put her hand on my shoulder. "I'm sorry I had to pretend to double-cross you."

I looked away and didn't say anything, still feeling hurt.

"I *had* to take you back to the poachers," she said. "If they thought you had gotten away, they would have radioed the yacht not to come in."

"You could have at least told me," I said, still not looking at her.

"I wanted to." Her voice sounded sad. "I really did. But I was afraid they might force you to talk. It was better if you really thought I was one of them."

"It's true, Eric C.," Sharon said. "She's been monitoring us all along."

"You know that belt she gave you?" Erik K. said.

I touched the leather belt around my waist.

"It's got a radio transmitter in it," Delia said. "We've kept track of you constantly."

"We met her when we were coming up the river just now, and she told us all about it," Sharon said.

"Will you forgive me, Eric C.?" Delia said.

I looked at her and nodded. "I'm sorry I didn't have more faith in you," I said. I thought about what Sharon had said—about all the dangers we had faced, and how each time God had provided a way out. Even when we felt helpless, and when there seemed to be nothing we could do. Even this last time.

Delia slipped an arm around my back and gave me a squeeze.

"But what are we going to do with the prisoners?" Erik said.

"No problem," Delia said. Pulling a walkie-talkie from her belt, she spoke into it. "This is Night Angel calling Screaming Meanie. Come in."

"This is Screaming Meanie, standing by," a man's voice replied.

"We've got three passengers who need a ride to the nearest jail, over."

"Ten-four. We're on our way. Out."

"What's Screaming Meanie?" Erik asked.

"A helicopter," Delia said. "It should be here in a few minutes." She glanced at Jake, Hubert, and the captain. "That'll give you men just enough time to name everybody involved in the poaching ring."

"We'll never talk," Jake growled.

Red Thunder took a step toward them. "We Calusas have other ways of dealing with people who don't respect our lands." As he drew his long hunting knife, I saw Hubert's eyes grow wide with fear.

Of course, I knew Red Thunder was bluffing—or was he?

21

Back home, Miss Spice treated us to a picnic at the state park, loading the table with delicious food. As we ate, ducks played on the nearby lake.

"Who's ready to go canoeing?" Miss Spice asked when we finished.

"Me!" we all said.

We walked down to the two canoes by the lake, put on our life vests, and pushed away from shore.

"What a lovely day!" said Miss Spice, who shared a boat with Sharon.

The sun shone brightly from a blue sky. A gentle breeze blew across the perfectly calm water.

"This sure beats paddling in a storm, with waves trying to swamp us," Erik said.

"And there aren't any mosquitoes or biting flies out here," Sharon added.

"I certainly am proud of you kids," Miss Spice said as we moved our boats side by side slowly across the lake. "You handled yourselves well in the Everglades. And I'm still amazed you were able to get the names of everyone in the poaching ring."

I grinned. "You can thank Red Thunder for that."

"What do you mean?"

"Well, when he pulled out his knife, the prisoners started talking. They told Delia everything she wanted to know."

"Yeah," Sharon said. "And the whole time, Red Thunder stood there cleaning his fingernails with the knife—and then he put it away."

We laughed.

"Well, you kids got through it all safely. That's the main thing. By the way, did you ever see any crocodiles or panthers?"

"No, ma'am," Sharon said. "Red Thunder said even he has never seen a crocodile, and he only saw a panther once, crossing a highway at night."

Miss Spice nodded. "Both of those are very rare. Maybe with these poachers behind bars, the Everglades will be a safer place for wildlife now."

"We did see the mama manatee and her baby again," Sharon said.

"How?"

"You know how after we got out of the swamp, we spent the night at Delia's house and got all cleaned up? Well, we had plenty of time the next day before our plane left, so she bought us tickets on an Everglades tour boat."

"It was more like a tour *bus*," Erik said. "It was all glassed in and air-conditioned, with a bunch of tourists."

"Sounds nice and comfy," said Miss Spice.

"Well, in a canoe you see lots more animals," Sharon said. "Anyway, we were passing the mouth of the Chatham River when a lady screamed, 'Sea monsters!'" Sharon giggled. "I looked out the window and there they were—the mama and her baby!"

"How wonderful!"

"I waved to them, and I think they saw me before they swam off."

"Oh, come on, Sharon—how could they recognize you through the windows?" Erik scoffed.

"Well, *I* think they did," she retorted.

"Anyway, it's good to know they're safe and sound," Miss Spice said. Then she added quietly, "For now."

We paddled into a quiet cove. Sharon yawned. Miss Spice set down her paddle. "This looks like a good place for a nap."

"A nap?" Erik said.

"Yeah, this water is as smooth as glass," Sharon said drowsily.

She and Miss Spice scooted around in their seats to find a comfortable position, settled their heads against the sides of the canoe, and closed their eyes.

Erik and I looked at each other. "Thought we came out here to paddle around, not sleep," he grumped.

I shrugged. To tell the truth, I was kind of sleepy myself. Something about the warm sun, the gentle rocking of the canoe—"Maybe we could rest for a minute or two," I said.

Miss Spice twisted in her seat again, then shook her head impatiently. "I can't quite get comfortable," she murmured sleepily. "Maybe if I stretch my legs out on this side and—"

Splash!

Sharon and Miss Spice rose sputtering from the waist-deep water, their canoe upside down.

Sharon wiped her eyes. "What happened?" she asked.

"I must have shifted my weight too much to one side," Miss Spice said, rubbing her face.

"Stop laughing!" Sharon commanded, but it was too late—Erik and I were completely out of control. And the fact that Sharon looked so mad at us made it even worse, remembering how she'd laughed at us when we'd capsized.

When he could speak again, Erik said, "Maybe you guys need some canoeing lessons."

Wringing the water from her hair, Sharon turned to Miss Spice and whispered, "Let's go dunk them."

But Erik and I moved quickly out of reach with a few strokes of our paddles. Then we stretched out, feet up, hands behind our heads.

"Guess you two better get over to the shore and empty your canoe," Erik said.

"Yeah," I said, closing my eyes. "And try not to wake us."